I pulled locks of hair over both cheeks, like heavy chains. My face was in shadow, but this girl had no fear of a stranger by his woodland fire. She drifted through the smoke towards me. My lamps had turned the forest into a glowing cave.

The girl wore a black top, with long sleeves and a V-neck. This gave a view of pale skin down to her small breasts. Her blue jeans were cut at the knees. She had a pair of muddy black boots with straggly laces.

As she came closer I saw a ring through her nose. Her platinum hair was dead straight and lay towards her chest. The fringe fell over her right eye.

I sat there spellbound as she stood before me. At last I said, 'Are you for real?'

She kicked me gently. 'Does that feel real?'

I shifted slightly, back into the shadow of Cherry's hut. 'Sure. Thing is, not many girls come this close to me.'

'Maybe you don't go close to them.'

'Maybe I've good reason not to.'

Also by Gareth Thompson

THE GREAT HARLEQUIN GRIM

SUNSHINE TO THE SUNLESS

THE ANARCHIST'S ANGEL

GARETH THOMPSON

DEFINITIONS

THE ANARCHIST'S ANGEL
A DEFINITIONS BOOK 978 1 909 53151 2

First published in Great Britain by Definitions,
an imprint of Random House Children's Books
A Random House Group Company

This edition published 2009

1 3 5 7 9 10 8 6 4 2

The Random House Group Limited supports The Forest Stewardship
Council® (FSC®), the leading international forest-certification organisation.
Our books carrying the FSC label are printed on FSC®-certified paper.
FSC is the only forest-certification scheme supported by the leading
environmental organisations, including Greenpeace. Our
paper procurement policy can be found at
www.randomhouse.co.uk/environment

Set in Palatino 11pt/16pt

Definitions are published by Random House Children's Books,
61–63 Uxbridge Road, London W5 5SA

www.**kids**at**randomhouse**.co.uk
www.**rbooks**.co.uk

Addresses for companies within The Random House Group Limited can be found at:
www.randomhouse.co.uk/offices.htm

THE RANDOM HOUSE GROUP Limited Reg. No. 954009

A CIP catalogue record for this book is available from the British Library.

Printed and bound in Great Britain by Clays Ltd, St Ives plc

Thanks to Dave Ward for good critique

ONE

I came round to the noise of a grim reaping machine. My left ankle felt like a scythe had cut through it. And the clatter of a giant red monster moved ever closer.

But then I remembered. This was all just a game, just a stupid, stupid game. I lay in a field full of evening sunshine. All around me were flies, rising from the barley like a plague of insects, each black dot hovering before the great sun.

I tried to move but waves of pain made me shudder. My ankle, my bloody ankle. It throbbed like a pulse, it burned like hot metal. And when I kicked the ground something ripped inside it, and another wave hit me.

My throat was parched, leaving me with no voice, and the machine rolled nearer. My stomach was a sick slop of terror.

Little grains shot into the air like sparks. Bees danced among them, as if drunk on summer's honey.

I heaved myself to one side and rolled over loose stones. But the barley lay thickly around me so I hardly moved.

The evening was a furnace, yet my bones were cold with shock. I managed to raise myself up on one elbow, my face deep in long and slender stems, all golden brown. Every stalk had tiny ears, with prickly hairs on the husks of each kernel. I tried to crawl, but my ankle dragged me back like a hot anvil.

That machine carved towards me, topping and tailing the harvest. It would spit me back out with the weeds. I was a boy sacrifice, an offering to this thing. Its blades were howling like a thousand demons, its engine roaring ever louder.

In those final moments I had only one thought. It was all my mum's fault. It was her who made me go to this bloody birthday party.

Two

Early that same day, Mum was pounding dough in the kitchen of our family's pub. A door stood open, letting in the drones of an August morning. Fat bees fizzed at the windows. Grasshoppers clicked and chirped outside.

Beyond our gravel car park, green hills were soaked with sunshine. Wolf Hill, in south Cumbria, was a heat-hazy country of fields and farms. The only sound of protest came from me, Samson Ashburner, aged ten. I tugged at Mum's apron.

'I don't wanna go to Mark Wilson's birthday,' I said. 'His big brother got me in the forest last week, and rubbed sheep's poo in my hair.'

Mum took her dough to the table, pulled off big chunks and rolled them. She spoke in her usual way, at top speed, so you had to listen hard.

'You must learn to stand up to Henry,' she said. 'Be big and brave like your name. The real Samson pushed over stone pillars.'

The real Samson lived a million years ago, when everyone had stupid names like mine. And the local kids called me Damson, not Samson, saying I was as

soft as fruit. Damson Ashburner. It was either that or
Tubby Tits.

My mum hurried around the kitchen. She was a big
and wheezy woman, cheeks like a greedy hamster's. She
wore large round glasses, and her flat hair was dyed a
dodgy orange colour. Everything was done in a furious
way, as if our pub was a top hotel. But even when summer
tourists flooded the other Lake District villages, we were
hardly rushed.

I stormed outside in a huff, across the car park, into the
kids' play area my mother had created. It lay in a clearing
in our lush orchard. An old metal garage stood at the near
edge, converted by Dad into his workshed.

I had only one thought in my mind. If I could break
an ankle, or even a leg, I'd get out of Mark Wilson's
party. Loads of kids from the Wolf Hill farms were
going, and none of them liked me – the porky pub boy,
not born of farming stock. It was time for the climbing
frame. The best chance to cause myself actual bodily
harm.

As my legs did battle with the wooden structure, my
lungs heaved for breath. 'Made it!' I gasped, standing at
the top like some bold explorer. I felt my chest bumping.
Maybe even a small heart attack would get me out of the
party! But as it gradually slowed, I knew it was time for
the last resort.

'Don't look down,' I whispered. 'Just jump.'

I held my nose like someone diving off the deep end,

and stepped into thin air. With eyes closed I waited for solid earth, and when my feet hit the ground I twisted and threw myself sideways. My left ankle took the full force, and the shooting pain that followed filled me with hope.

'Help!' I shouted. 'Dad! I'm hurt.'

He came running out of his shed, wearing greasy overalls. You could see who I got my curly black hair and round belly from. Dad's nose had been a bit wonky ever since a drunken customer lamped him with an iron poker kept in the front bar.

'Easy, Sam,' he said. 'Try and walk it off.'

I stood with a groan. 'I can't go to the party now. You'll have to tell Mum.' With a dramatic stumble I fell on my knees, facing the orchard. Then a shadow passed over me. A fast and screechy voice came with it.

'He'll tell me nothing like it,' said my mother. 'You'll go to that party if I have to take you in the wheelbarrow. You've been invited by the Wilsons and you'll jolly well go. And you'll run around with the others too. Do some exercise. Work up a sweat. You've been under my feet for weeks, stuffing your face in my kitchen. Now get up and get busy.'

She stomped back into the pub, giving my father a glare through giant round specs. 'Honest,' I complained. 'My ankle really hurts.'

Dad gave a helpless shrug and walked away. 'Sorry, son,' he said. 'You know who's in charge here.'

As I sat down angrily, my hand landed on the remains of a sticky lollipop in the grass. It was covered with a swarm of ants. I waited for my mother to get back indoors, then flung it after her. I half-shouted, 'Suck on that, you ... you ... you ...'

THREE

By early afternoon my ankle had begun to swell. I rolled down a sock and went into the kitchen to show Mum.

'Look!' I wailed. 'It's busted.'

'Cover that smelly foot up, and get ready to walk down to the farm,' Mum yakked back. I often found it hard to catch every word she hurled out. It was like standing under a shower and trying to see each separate droplet.

She shuffled around the kitchen on flat feet, bottom wobbling like a cartoon duck. At the big stove, among pans and bubbling pots, she turned sharply. 'Hands off those raspberries. They're for summer puddings, and you didn't get up early enough to come and pick them. Now put clean clothes on and be ready in five minutes.'

Shortly after, I was limping beside her down the lane. Wolf Hill wasn't a village in the sense of shops and streets. The area was just a collection of farms, with a few big houses for rich outsiders. In fact, the only place you could buy food or drink was at The Forge. The building dated back to 1750, and still had wooden beams and stone-flagged floors. Even before it was a pub people had gathered here, when there'd been a blacksmith working next door.

The hedges on both sides were sky-high. It was cool in their shade; shelter from the exploding sun.

'Stop dragging your feet,' said Mum. 'It's like walking with a leper.'

'That's horrible. Lepers have bodies that fall to bits.'

'You'll fall to bits soon. Get a move on.'

We carried on down the steep lane, past an old cottage that used to be a small factory making bobbins for Lancashire cotton mills. Its walls were covered by heaps of thick ivy. Only the windows were visible, two upstairs and two downstairs. It was like a four-eyed monster, with a door for the mouth, peeping out from shaggy green fur.

The hedges gave way to drystone walls, and the valley opened up on our left. Lime-green meadows were dotted with farm buildings.

We stopped by a gap in the wall. 'Squeeze through there,' said Mum. 'Then run down to the farm and take this present for Mark. And behave: remember to say thank you.'

Down on my left was the Wilson place, with its metal barn. In the summer calm you could hear the squeals and shouts of playing children. The party was already in full swing.

I took the wrapped-up gift and tried to squeeze through a break in the wall. 'I can't,' I gasped, edging sideways. 'I'll have to climb over, even with a bust ankle.'

But my mum hadn't time to indulge me. She stepped

back, then gave me a shoulder barge through the gap that would've done a sumo wrestler proud.

'And don't be back before eight,' she said. Standing there like a guard, she watched me trudge across the grass. I made a big show of limping, and forcing a way through the far hedge.

Wilson's barn stood at the near edge of the field. Everything had the hot and shitty smell of a farm in August. Cows mooed away like grumpy grandmas.

The barn had no covering at the front or back, and I could see everyone inside playing a loud version of Musical Chairs. A portable CD blasted out something dancey, as the party kids charged around trying to sit on bales of hay. When the game ended they came racing out and piled into each other.

Everyone stopped when they saw me. They wore wellies, like farm children always seem to, even in town. Mark Wilson, the birthday brat, had sandy hair and rubbery lips. He looked at the present I held.

'What's that?'

'For you,' I said, handing it over.

He ripped off the wrapping and flung it on the grass. Then came a chorus of groans and laughs as a stupid toy tractor appeared. A tiny farmer sat in the driver's seat.

'Oh, wow! Do we all get one?'

'Any plastic piggies to go with it?'

'I'd so rather have that than an Xbox.'

'It's brill! Look, its little wheels even go round.'

'Cheers, Damson,' said Mark. 'I'm actually eleven today, not three.' He led the gang back and I followed miserably like a pig to the butcher's. Another game started up, but I could hardly move on my stiff ankle. Whenever the music stopped there was nowhere for me to sit down, yet everyone else somehow had a straw bale to crash on.

At last an adult shouted and it seemed that tea was ready. The farmhouse stood further up behind a thicket of trees. We kicked off our boots and all ran indoors to be first.

Mrs Wilson, tough and tiny, had laid on a spread. A pink ham, crusty bread, white and yellow cheeses, leafy salads, strawberry tarts, and a birthday cake with chocolate icing and eleven candles. Everyone piled their plates and ran in smelly socks to the front room.

I sat alone, tucked up in the corner scoffing my grub. The others were watching some gormless DVD with a robot-killer zapping humans. I kept slipping out for more food, pouring burpy lemonade into my glass.

When the film finally ended I was yawning and stuffed. A noise of machinery starting up came drifting in from outside. Mark Wilson, his chin pointed like a pixie, stood on a chair to look out, then jumped off with a cunning grin. 'Blind Baxter's driving the combine,' he said. 'So, it's time to play Death in the Barley! Who's in, or who's too chicken?'

'I'm in! I'm in!'

'Yeah! Yeah!'

Mark punched his palm. 'Cool,' he said. 'Let's go, gang.'

Four

I'd seen this game happening before, and was glad it had never involved me. But soon we were all outside again. High overhead a falcon hovered, and twitched its wings like a dark angel.

Above the Wilson farm lay the edge of Appletree Wood, a thick and ancient forest. It ran eastwards as you faced the trees, in a long ridge. The pastures below it were mostly green, but one large golden field shone out among the grasslands.

We lurked in bushes at the edge of this barley meadow. It was a long rectangular field. A combine harvester stood at the far end, its driver poking about in the machinery.

The sun was glowing onto granite hills beyond Appletree Wood. A flock of birds flew from the forest and we all looked up at the sudden flutter.

I said, 'I own that woodland. The whole lot.'

The other kids gave big snorts. 'Yeah, right,' said Henry Wilson, Mark's older brother by a year. He was all sandy hair and muscles. 'You don't own anything, except the pub that nobody goes to.'

'Honest,' I boasted. 'My great-grandpa was called

Charcoal Cherry, and he owned Appletree. It's worth millions of pounds, and now it's mine.'

Everyone howled at this. Molly Hatton blew dark hair from her rosy face, then kicked my bum with a dirty wellie. 'If you Ashburners are so rich,' she said, 'why don't you live in a proper house?'

'We live in the pub,' I protested.

This brought more wails of laughter. I gave a stupid smile.

'You all live in the pub's top rooms, 'cos you can't afford a proper house.'

'Do you all share a bed up there?'

'Yeah, I bet they do. Samson sleeps with his mummy.'

'We all know why your great-grandpa was called Charcoal Cherry. He sat burning his stupid fires, and drank himself to death on cherry brandy.'

I shouted, 'Shut up, Mark! And you! All of you!'

In a rage I tried to run at Molly, but my ankle gave way and I fell over near her feet. She rubbed a mucky boot in my hair. I punched her leg and she jumped on my back. 'I'll pull your trousers down,' she shouted. 'I will.'

I was saved by the combine harvester revving up. Molly got off me and sneered, 'Is old Blind Baxter still driving?'

Mark said, 'He ain't totally blind yet.'

Henry chipped in. 'He's been mowing that field over forty years. Dad reckons he could do it in the dark.'

'Yeah,' said Suzy Dixon, the one I thought of as Pig

Face. 'We can play Death in the Barley without him seeing us.'

Bright sunlight still lit the thick rows of barley. Each stalk seemed to flame alive, ready for the chop.

The mechanical monster driven by Blind Baxter came towards us, chomping down the field's near edge. Mark and Henry crawled quickly into the barley, and we watched as they pushed their way through. The red machine was almost upon them when they leaped away, just out of the combine's reach, and into the dense barley on the other side.

Everyone cheered and whooped, but I was horrified. The sad saps thought this was cool and were expecting me to play too.

Molly turned to me and said, 'You'd better not back out. I'll tell everyone at big school when we start in September.' Her brown eyes had sussed my fear.

'Got a bad ankle,' I mumbled.

'Chicken licken.'

'Lesbian.'

'You what? Say that again, Tubby Tits.'

Molly was a sturdy girl, a real farmer's lass. She brought her own daily pint of raw milk to junior school, and downed it in one at break time. 'Fresh this morning,' she'd say. 'Squeezed the tits myself.'

She reached out, grabbed me firmly, and with one shove I was into the field. 'Get running,' she said. 'You'd better do at least three leaps, or your pants come down.'

I got on my knees and crept into the golden jungle. I raised myself to see Baxter still bearing down the sloping field, and threw myself out of his path.

'Cheat!' Molly shouted. 'You weren't in line with it.'

I wished the combine would chew her up and spurt her bloody guts out of its funnel. I tried to lose myself in the barley again, sneezing with dust and grains. Somebody punched me on the arm, giving me a fright. It was Henry Wilson, his biceps like boxing gloves.

'Lose yourself, Ashburner. This is my hideout.'

'OK. Let me sit down a mo.'

'You've got two seconds, Damson.'

'Right. Hey, Henry, you think Molly's a lesbian?'

Henry yelped like he'd been stung. 'You freak! Molly Hatton rocks and she's well fit. Lesbians look more like your mum.'

'OK, OK,' I said, wiping my brow. 'I'll be off.'

'Good. You don't even know what a lesbian is.'

'I do.'

'What then?'

I wasn't really sure and I was being mobbed by midges. I began hobbling to the far border of the big field, out of Henry's way. There was an enormous stack of black plastic sacks up there. I stooped through a sea of barley to the top left corner, where they stood.

The combine stopped, and when I looked over to see what was happening, Baxter had got out to adjust the height of its roller. Maybe it was getting blunted on the hidden rocks. Then I was off again, my ankle playing hell.

At last I lay against one of the sacks to rest up. They were all full of hay for animal feed in the winter. The summer evening was filled with the joyful shouts of children, as they played at dicing with death. I closed my eyes and had a few moments of peace, even dozing off for a bit.

Then some idiot was shouting my name. 'Ashburner! Where are you?' It was Henry Wilson. I wasn't gonna get away so easily.

I stood up on my good ankle. 'Over here!' I shouted, keeping a close eye on the combine. It was homing in on me, the sun glinting off its body.

I tried to hop through the dense crops before me . . . managed a quick dash . . . and that's when it happened! I slipped on a dirty great hidden rock. Something twisted in my stiff ankle, something ripped open. A flame of pain seared through me. I screamed once, and blacked out before I even hit the ground.

Much later, I filled in those blank seconds. Henry Wilson heard me shriek and stumbled his way through to me.

'Get up!' He shook me hard and tried to drag my weight away. 'Mark! Molly! I can hardly move him.'

Molly fought through the barley, shouting at the kids behind her. 'Stop Baxter! Stop him!' She leaped onto the black sacks, trying to grip their shiny plastic. Baxter was maybe one minute away, his combine mowing up the field's left edge towards me. Molly was pulling and tugging the sacks.

Henry leaped out of the barley, then ran down a furrow between the crops and the fence. He sprinted in his wellies and jumped onto the combine's footplate. He yelled at the driver, banging the window. 'Get the brakes on! Do it! Get the brakes on!'

I came back round to pain and panic. Baxter had taken a swerve to avoid that heap of black sacks, but this led him right into my path.

As the combine loomed, I could almost feel its burning blades and their hot prongs. There was a groan of brakes.

And then from overhead, black plastic cylinders came tumbling down. Molly Hatton was pulling those sacks of hay into the combine's path. As the harvester skidded and slowed, I curled into a ball like something unborn.

The sacks pushed me backwards, shoved by the braking combine. But the machine still had enough power to cut through them. Dry grass went spurting everywhere. Another huge plastic roll fell and hurt me.

As the combine's blades stopped rolling, they cut into the last sacks. The spikes and my head were both covered in hay.

I felt slashes of heat on my face, like burning snakes' tongues, or a garden rake that's been forged in fire. The wetness of blood filled my eyes and mouth. An unnatural silence settled over everything, and all I knew were two things: I was alive, but I was mangled in some way.

I tried getting to my feet but fell back, one ankle screaming. The crowd of birthday kids was breathless with shock, looking down on me.

Molly wailed and covered her eyes. Henry coughed his guts up. Guilt was carved into everyone's face, but even then I knew this was down to one person. Mum.

And that's when my slide into solitude began.

FIVE

It was the morning of my last day at secondary school. Five summers had passed since that gruesome game of Death in the Barley.

I stood in the bathroom of our living quarters above The Forge pub. Lifting my wet face from the sink I met a familiar sight in the mirror.

Samson Ashburner, aged fifteen, nearly sixteen. Over six feet tall now and quite brawny. I had lost my kiddie belly and taken on hard muscle. My black hair was curly in a long and untidy tumble. I'd grown it thick, so that only my eyes, mouth and nose were visible. But even this couldn't hide all the red marks, and time hadn't helped that much. Both my eyebrows were in separate parts, each with a notch of bare skin down the middle.

It looked like I'd been pressing my face against thin metal bars. Five years locked in a hell of my mother's making.

A month after the incident at Wilson's farm, I was thrown into life at big school, with hundreds of new strangers to stare at me. Around each corner were girls whose own unscarred beauty made me go weak.

'Here comes Red Stripe,' I'd hear them say, like I was deaf as well.

'Red Stripe at night, shepherd's delight!'

I sat at the back of every classroom, out of sight. Girls were like the moon and the stars to me – far beyond my reach, but shining so bright.

So, on the morning of my final GCSE, one thing was certain. There was no question of me going on to sixth-form college, to face another wave of staring beauties. I'd make damn sure I failed this exam too, as I'd surely failed my others.

I had taken to wearing a baseball cap and hooded top to shade my face, and a large pair of sunglasses. Leaving the pub, I turned left up the lane. The hedgerows buzzed with life and wafted sweet perfumes. Summer was already a season of drowsy lust.

My black T-shirt was moist with sweat. It bore the logo PRODUCT OF A BROKEN HOME. I rated it as my mother's fifth least favourite shirt of mine.

I looked back over the green and golden valley. Red-brick buildings and barns were way down to the left like models on a toy farm. Looming above them was the edge of Appletree Wood. From here the trees looked like dark green broccoli, all crammed together. Behind this thick wood were the lower slopes of Stickle Pike. The mountain summit was a grey wart, standing above the jagged peaks behind it to the west.

The woodland was my freedom, my sanctuary; every-where else felt like chains.

At the top of the steep lane was a wooden sign, hidden

under tangled growth, as if nature was trying to discourage visitors. Its two carved words, obscured by moss, pointed back down to the place we lived – Wolf Hill.

As the school bus appeared, I jammed on my iPod with some dreamy drum 'n' bass. I got on board without a word or a glance, and took my place on the corner of the back seat. No one else had dared sit there for years. It was where moody Red Stripe always sat.

'You may turn over your papers and begin.'

In the sweaty school hall I got ready to flunk my final exam. It was English, and we were meant to write about *Macbeth*, but instead I penned an essay on *Lord of the Rings*. I discussed Tolkien's use of nature and tree studies, gave myself an A* below it, then sat admiring Mary Degdale at the next desk.

I began with her bare feet, which she'd slipped out of her trainers. She wore a short white skirt. Her eyes were green, her red-brown hair awash with sunshine. Finally she sensed my stare, then fixed me with a blank look, tapping a pen on her swan-like neck. 'What?' she mouthed silently.

I mouthed back, 'You look nice.'

Mary pointed two fingers down her throat, and returned to *Macbeth*.

You could only find comfort in nature – I had learned that by now. So when the exam was over, and me not wanting to face the canteen, I headed for the nearby lake. Turning right at the school gates I joined the tourists going to Coniston Water. I wore my baseball cap, hooded top and sunglasses.

The cap had a slogan on it: OH GREEN WORLD! The make of the zip-up hoodie was Dark Zone. And my specs were a standard pair of big shades.

So, I'd given these three items names . . . Green, Dark & Shady. It made them sound like members of an eco-rap band, and it also described the woodland I hung out in back home. I hardly went anywhere without my disguises, and only took them off in school to sit with head in hands.

Coniston got rammed in high summer. The village was hemmed in by cloudy mountains, with its lake of deep mystery. Houses of grey slate and white stone lay in the shadow of brooding brown hills. I knew the scenes were really awesome and everything, but it also felt like the fag end of nowhere. A place to dream yourself away from at fifteen, nearly sixteen.

I crunched over to a bench which gave a view down the lake's blue throat. A five-mile stretch of Coniston Water lay ahead, dotted with sails like giant white fins. On the far side of the lake, trees sloped up into the distance, making a forest of jungle green.

Nearby on the pebbled shore, a large Asian family had gathered. Maybe they'd driven up from Lancashire for the day. About a dozen of them, all ages, were talking and laughing in white robes. They'd also brought their own cooking gear, and big camping stoves blew hot gas at steel pots. Sweet and spicy smells filled the fresh air.

I was hungry, and closed my eyes to dream of exotic food. My belly rumbled as I dozed, and when I opened my eyes a little Asian boy stood before me, with a paper plate full of curry and rice. He smiled shyly and offered it to me.

I was eager for food and human warmth. Without thinking, I took off my glasses and swept my hair aside. 'Is that for me? Wow, that's really kind.'

The smile dropped from his golden-brown face, and he backed away slowly.

'It's OK,' I called out. 'Don't be scared.'

But the sight of my scars had been too much, and that sweet kid ran off crying, slopping curry onto the shore. I put Green, Dark & Shady all firmly back into place.

To celebrate the end of exams, the school had invited a local Body Shop to do makeovers in the hall. Boys slapped on aftershave, and girls shrieked at the sight of new nail polish. Everyone got high on their own manicured beauty.

I stood with my face to the windows, looking in at the vanity parade. Then of course someone had to go and spoil it, and as usual it was Mabel Johnson. I watched as this great cuckoo crashed over to the lipstick stand. Her face was white and round like a toilet bowl. But today she'd streaked her cheeks with red marks, and was lumbering around the room with hands in pockets.

I heard her shout, 'Guess who?' A few people forced a laugh.

'Go on,' she shouted again. 'Guess who?'

Someone nudged her and nodded at the windows. Mabel turned and her cold little eyes met mine. I stuck two fingers up at her, but she just shrugged her meaty shoulders and turned away. The room went quiet until I slunk off like a public enemy, and heard the screeching start up again.

So secondary school ended for me about the same way as it began.

Six

Early that evening, I lay festering in my room above The Forge.

A knock at the door. 'Dad?' I said.

'No,' said Mum. 'It's me.'

I groaned, and got up to face her.

Mum tried pushing the door wide but I blocked it. 'Get that mess cleaned up,' she said, looking inside. 'It's a right old scrow.'

'Yeah, right. Anything else?'

'Yes. What happened in your English exam?'

'What d'you mean?'

'I mean, was it easy, will you have passed?'

'Yep. You get an A just for smiling.'

'Don't be stupid, Samson. You know the results are published in the local paper. I'd rather you didn't bring disgrace on the family.'

I tried shutting the door, but Mum wedged a fat foot in.

'Owt else?' I asked.

'Yes. You'll have to work in the kitchen this summer, so get a haircut. Right?'

'Whateva.' I slammed the door, and got ready to visit my woodland hideaway.

*

Nobody knows the true origins of Appletree Wood. The forest was probably an orchard in ancient times but there are no exact records of the place. It could have begun as a fruit farm, almost unique among the region's cattle and crop lands. Some think it was run by a medieval tribe of outsiders and outcasts. Maybe they talked of peace or revolution, among the quinces and pears.

But one thing I know for certain: hazel branches were burned in Appletree Wood to make charcoal. My great-grandpa, Cherry Ashburner, was among the last of these workers. Cherry was a loner, who stayed living in Appletree long after the charcoal days. He slept rough, and brewed his own cherry brandy. The wood has been cut back since his time, but it's still thick and spooky, and I could wander a long time there without fear of company.

It included a dense copse that I loved, above Wilson's farm. I was really proud of owning it. Yep, that's right, I really did own it, and it came about because of Cherry and the local landowner back then.

Lord Henry Harker named his grand house after himself. Harker Hall stands off a narrow lane leading out of Wolf Hill. Across from its driveway are meadows, that barley field, and then Appletree Wood beyond.

Henry Harker was a wild card, fond of hunting and high living. He was even said to feed his hounds on caviar and champagne. But he would also dress like a beggar, to wander among Cumbrian villages as an unknown.

Cherry and Henry had a document drawn up. It partly refers to the wooden wigwam built by Cherry in Appletree Wood, where he used to stay during the long charcoal burns. This is what the old piece of paper says, and it bears the Harker crest.

It is agreed from this day, the following matter between
Lord Henry Harker and Charles 'Cherry' Ashburner.
That the woodland around Mr Ashburner's hut, namely
Appletree Wood, be gifted to him by Lord Harker.

Upon Charles Ashburner's death, this woodland shall
be handed down to the youngest of the family. This
will come to pass on the day of the child's birth. In so
doing, we shall always keep the woodland alive with
innocent joys. This all rests upon one condition: that the
Ashburners continue to supply their cherry brandy to the
Harkers of Harker Hall.

So decrees Lord Henry Harker and Mr Charles 'Cherry'
Ashburner. And may God have mercy upon our noble
souls.

The document is signed by both men. So as the youngest and only child in our family I became a property owner, even if I only got a woodland full of sad squirrels.

But there's something else I inherited from Cherry. In the past few years I had hooked into the whole charcoal-burning thing myself, after doing plenty of research. It's a quiet and lonely task, so you get to spend hours away from everyone. You also get the smell of woodsmoke, like nature's own joss-stick. And after another day of hard knocks at school, I needed my special place.

I was on my way up there, when Dad shouted.

'Samson? Hang on there, son.'

He came out of his rusty old shed, where he was trying to create his own beers, to save him having to buy from other local makers. Plans for this were quite advanced, except for one crucial thing. The god-awful beer itself.

He came sweating towards me with a half-pint glass and passed it over. I held it to the sunlight. It looked like he'd already drunk the brew himself, peed it back into the glass, and stirred in some dodgy pond life.

I sniffed. It smelled like the gents' toilet block at Silecroft beach.

I took a cautious sip. Something like you'd imagine the juice at the bottom of wheelie bins.

'You're getting better at it,' I lied.

Dad took the glass back. 'You think so? Not too malty?'

'Nah. If anything, I'd chuck some more in. Roast it first, like.'

'Right. Yeah. You off to your wood?'

'Yep. See you later.'

I strode away, wearing Green, Dark & Shady. Dad called after me. 'Samson? About next term. About you doing a catering course at college . . .'

'Not now, Dad. Later.'

I had this plan for getting out of sixth-form college, with its fresh packs of girls to scorn and pity me. If I got my own charcoal business going, I could live among the leaves like a baby gorilla.

I might even do up Cherry's old hut and make it really habitable. My main hope was a local heritage fund I'd written to, with full details of my business plans. I'd had a letter from them, thanking me for my proposal, so now I was waiting to see if they shared my vision.

I headed down the lane, then up an old cart track. This led past the Wilson farm on the left and uphill into Appletree Wood.

With no strangers or tourists about, I dumped Green, Dark & Shady, and switched off my mobile. Then I was free again in my own quiet kingdom.

Seven

I entered a dark mass of pines, where sunlight slanted through and each trunk was hooped with shadows. Hazel trees grew like spindly ostrich legs.

Leading through this green maze was a rough path. It went deep into Appletree Wood and stopped near Cherry's hut. His old shelter looked a bit like a grassy wigwam. Its frame was built with tall poles, tied together at the top. The spaces in between were filled with slabs of clay and mud, then covered by ferns and bracken.

An opening was left at the front to face the charcoal-burning site. Inside I'd built a simple bed of springy brushwood and straw. My grubby sleeping bag lay on it. There was a layer of carpet on the floor that I'd nabbed from a farm skip.

An old tin box lay hidden inside under dried ferns. It was my stash tin for everything from a girly mag I found in the pub's bottle bins, to my copy of Cherry's old document. The box was the size of a large atlas, with a handle at either end, and weighed a bloody ton. This hefty thing might have been Cherry's too, as I unearthed it not far from his hut, when preparing the ground for charcoal burning.

In the eighteenth century, boats on nearby Coniston Water shipped out charcoal from this region. It was used to extract metal from ore, because it heats to such a high temperature. The Romans even used it to forge swords and body armour. Nowadays people want it for barbecues, or drawing.

But I liked burning charcoal as a way to lose myself in a more ancient world. And the smoky black smears it made covered the marks on my face.

Inside Cherry's old hut was a pile of hazel branches. With my billhook blade I cut them into lengths of about a metre, then used it to peel away the bark.

I kept a very old photo of Cherry. He was resting with his back to a drystone wall. He wore rough working clothes and held the same curving billhook that I had inherited. Under a top hat, his lined face looked bronzed. His beard was biblical, his eyes glaring like a tiger's.

I often thought of his restless spirit, still roaming the wood. 'Final day of exams,' I said to him. 'Not that you ever bothered with school. Too busy off scavenging.'

Too busy stealing hearts, my boy. Breaking them or bruising them, with any game girl.

'Yeah? Send one my way. Make sure she doesn't mind a long-haired loon, with a face like a burned zebra.'

Don't clout yourself over the lasses. You'll find one soon enough. Now get a load of charcoal firing, and make this woodland glow.

'Will do, Cherry. You mad old goat.'

To make charcoal, you need an area of level ground called the pitstead. In winter, when the overgrowth dies, you can still see traces of these in Cumbrian woodlands.

I put the hazel sticks in piles, onto my pitstead. It was very small, not like the huge circles that were once cleared for commercial use. I burned tiny amounts that were done in hours, not days. But over the summer I was going to make the pitstead much wider and rounder, in case I got a backer for my charcoal scheme.

I laid out the hazel like the spokes of a wheel, piling it up in layers. Then I covered it all with turf and bracken, to keep the heat inside and the air out. It looked like a big beehive with its little dome shape. I left a hole at the centre, and poured some burning wood down it. This began the whole slow process.

Before long, I saw damp patches on the earthy covering. With the combustion under way, I closed the chimney hole with a sod of grass, then I was free to sit in the doorway to Cherry's hut. I jammed on the iPod, wrapped myself in some rappy pop tune about love and windmills, and sat back to brood.

So that's how we passed our time together, me and my charcoal stack. We would often sit and smoulder as one. Both of us burning away slowly inside.

*

After a while, white smoke began to curl from the mound. There was a clearing around the pitstead, 'cos nothing could grow on the scorched and ashy ground, and decades of smoke had killed off any tree growth overhead. The fumes drifted freely to the sky through this natural chimney. From high above you could see right down to Cherry's hut.

Night fell over the woodland, bringing the scurry of small creatures. I lit two of Cherry's old oil lamps that now had candles inside. They hung off the nearest branches like glowing owls.

Grabbing one of my tin buckets, I stomped away to a nearby stream. It ran the full length of Appletree Wood, coming down from a mountain spring up in the hills towards Stickle Pike. I scooped water from the brook which was down to a trickle in the drought, and took it back to the pitstead.

I removed part of the earth covering on the stack, and poured in the water. This helped to smother the charcoal. I replaced the earth, to let everything cool right down.

'Nearly done, Cherry,' I said. 'Reckon I'm a master at it now.'

Shut yer moy, lad! It teks years to be a master burner.

'I reckon years is what I've got. Nowt else planned but this.'

Aye, and that's a shame. Too lonely a life for a young lad.

'I don't mind. Who needs company?'

Three hours after I'd started it, the burn was finished. I kicked away the turf and let the charcoal get some air. My clothes were smoky, my boots blackened. Using a big old sieve with a wooden border, I sifted the charcoal bits to remove earth and dust. It's a fine and filthy process so my face got nicely smeared. No trace of red stripes just then.

It made enough to fill one shopping bag and I stashed it in Cherry's hut along with some others. So far, our pub was the only taker for the fruits of my labour, when Mum fired up the barbie.

Then I rested in the doorway and meditated. Hot cinders floated like fireflies.

I closed my eyes, and inhaled the scents of the charcoal burn. I'd brought some potatoes to cook in the ashes, and was dreaming of hot food when a cracking twig snapped me awake. It was a human sound; too careless for animal paws. I glared across the smoky pitstead into the forest gloom. A shadow shifted and I got a glimpse of something pale, or of long white hair. I fumbled for Green, Dark & Shady. Soft footsteps went running back along the path.

'Who's that?' I shouted, but no one answered. I crossed over to a crop of hazel stalks where the intruder had lurked. I knew every sniff and scent of this wood, and there was a new aroma; the exciting tingle of a girl's perfume. Maybe a sweet hint of her sweat too.

Nothing like the pong of Wolf Hill's farm girls, this was the smell of a total stranger. I breathed her wild musk in deeply.

Eight

'Samson!' my mother shrieked. 'You stink like a smoked kipper!'

'Thanks. Smell quite funky yourself.'

'I needed your help in the kitchen hours ago. No need to ask where you were.'

'Don't ask then.'

'Right, well, when you've washed your filthy face, you can start on these pots.'

With a grunt of disgust, I hauled myself up the back stairs. Our living quarters were above the pub, although space was limited. It was like a flat, with two bedrooms and a bathroom. The wallpaper was yellow and peeling. There was a tiny spare bedroom, but over the years no brothers or sisters arrived to fill it, so it became the pub's office. I remained the family's youngest child, and the owner of Appletree Wood.

I slowly washed off my dark disguise before the bathroom mirror, and gently rubbed the redness below. There'd been no compensation for an accident that no one took the blame for. My mother seemed to pretend it never happened, as if anything was better than thinking about that wretched birthday party. We both retreated into our separate lives – hers in the pub kitchen and mine in Appletree Wood.

Back downstairs, Mum stood picking peel and muck from the sink. Dad came through, now the pub was closed for the night, sounding excited. 'Guess what? Someone's moved into Harker Hall at last.' It had been on the market for ages.

'How much ackers did they pay?' I said. 'Asking millions, weren't they?'

'No one knows,' said Dad. 'First time the Harker family hasn't been the owners. Old Lord Henry must be turning in his grave.'

Mum bashed sticky mush off her garlic press. 'So we've got a new lord of the manor,' she yapped. 'We'd best get round there, make a good impression, and get them to bring their rich friends here for dinner.'

Dad said, 'All in good time, love. Let them settle in first.'

But there was to be no settling in for the wealthy new neighbours. Nor did my mother grant me a lie-in on my first day of freedom from schooling.

A bang at my door. 'Samson! Get up. Your working life starts today!'

I took my time getting ready and chose a T-shirt

that said, THANK YOU FOR POT SMOKING. I rated it as Mum's fourth least favourite of mine.

Downstairs, she poured coffee and snorted. 'Must you wear that vile top?'

'Oh, I must.'

'And must you sit out in the wood all night, burning charcoal? The whole world talks about your strange behaviour.'

'No, Mother. I don't think some little Eskimos fishing by an ice hole in Greenland are having debates about a boy from Wolf Hill. Charcoal burning is a rare and ancient craft. Try giving that some thought.'

The table took the brunt of Mum's fist. 'And when will you start giving some thought to things? Like doing a catering course at Barrow College next term? Then you might be of some real use around the place.'

I stood up, scraping my chair on the flagstones. 'I'm not going to Barrow. I've got my own plans for a charcoal business. I want out of this whole stupid system.'

Mum started grinding her teeth and wheezing from the chest. 'It'll never happen,' she said. 'Do you really expect to compete with cheap supermarket bags of charcoal? You're a silly dreamer and it's time you started getting real.' She leaned against the table, looking worn-out.

'Well, pardon me for being born,' I said. 'And having a mind of my own.' I stomped upstairs to the office, and took down a box from the top shelf. I whipped out my birth certificate, then went back to wave it at Mum.

'What's that?'

'My birth certificate. Shall I give it a nice cremation?' I grabbed the toaster, slid the sheet in, and pulled the handle. 'There. Now it's like I never happened.'

'Samson!' Mum screamed. 'Get that thing out of there!' She rushed over and yanked the paper as its corners began scorching. 'For pity's sake!'

She sat down at the table, head in hands. The heavy wheezing started over like her lungs were full of cobwebs. I went back upstairs with my birth certificate and stared at it again.

Name – Samson Marcus Ashburner

Born – August 24th

Parents – Peter & Carol Ashburner

Occupation of father – Publican

I managed a laugh at my birth weight. A solid twelve pounds. I was a right blobber back then. And what a gayass name to begin life with. Samson!

I never asked my parents why they'd not had more kids. But living at such close quarters, I'd probably have known if they were still trying.

*

I lay on my unmade bed with my iPod, listening to a mix called Rain Forest Echoes. A flyer for The Forge was slipped under my door.

'Samson,' came Mum's voice. 'Take this to Harker Hall. And try to be polite.'

Our flyers were made of folded coloured card. The cover showed the pub's whitewashed front and grey slate roof. Inside were photos of our fireplace lined with copper pots, and the dining area with its low beams. Info about the pub's ancient origins, the beer range, and Mum's use of local produce were included. With us owning the pub there was no big brewery to bail us out, or buy us out. Hidden away as we were, we had to fight for every customer, and Wolf Hill had no easy tourist attractions.

I put on Green, Dark & Shady, then skulked down the lane, heading right at the old ivy cottage. Further along the narrow road was a turning to Harker Hall. For years the place had been unlived in, except for visits from Harker relatives. It was more of a large grey townhouse than a stately manor. Beech trees lined the avenue like sentries.

To the hall's left was a high stone wall, with a wide archway, and outbuildings beyond. Flyer in hand, I went down to the main front door. A babble of voices came from within. It sounded like a right slanging match. I heard a shrill scream that must have been a woman's. Furious words went flying back and forth. That scream rang out again. A door slammed, then another, and I heard footsteps running around the back. There was a crash of smashed glass.

I was about to turn away and leg it when the door suddenly opened.

NINE

'Hello? What do you want?'

I stared at a beautiful woman. She was maybe about my mother's age, but the contrast was dazzling. She wore a silk scarf and elegant pink suit. No fast and squeaky voice either. This lady spoke with high society dripping from her glossed lips.

Her hair was long and blonde, with a darkish crown. Her forehead was clear and creamy. Both eyebrows were golden and pencil-thin. Maybe her nose was a touch too sharp, with slim nostrils. But the skin was still tight around her cheekbones. I was blown away by such mature beauty.

'I'm from The Forge,' I said. I peeped past her for any signs of the recent quarrel.

'From the what?'

'The Forge,' I said, handing over the flyer. 'The local pub.'

She took the coloured leaflet. 'I see. Do you know where the nearest Sainsbury's is? An M & S, perhaps?'

'Oh, um, right down in Lancaster,' I said. 'You've a Co-op in Coniston though, and a good bakery in Broughton.'

She gave me a sorrowful stare. And as I burned under this gaze, I got a whiff of mysterious perfume. It somehow kept me there, breathing it in and talking.

'Are you here for good?' I asked.

'Possibly. It looks quite suitable.'

A door thumped inside, sounding louder now the front one was open. Then two little kiddies came squirming past and ran into the driveway.

'Be careful, twins,' called the lady. 'And don't go any further than the gate.'

I laughed. 'You're in Wolf Hill now. Safe as eggs in a hen.' I watched those two brats, a girl and a boy, messing around on the lawn. When I looked back at the woman, she was peering at herself in the front window. She rubbed the faint lines around her eyes and brushed up her eyelashes. I decided to sneak away as she gazed at her reflection.

'I'll be off,' I said.

'What? Oh, of course.' She stepped towards me. 'What heavy clothes you wear, young man. Aren't you hot?'

'Nah. I'm OK.'

'You cut a strong figure. Why not push all that hair aside, let the sunshine in?'

A man's posh voice boomed from indoors. 'Celia! Where's my bloody BlackBerry?'

The lady edged back inside. 'Nice to meet you . . . Mr . . . ?'

'Ashburner,' I said. 'Samson Ashburner.'

'How sweet. I am Lady Standish. My husband is Lord Hugo Standish.'

She said it like I was meant to faint in awe. Later that day I went on the internet, and found out that Standish was some rich big shot in property development. He and his wife had been 'happily married for twenty years', the report said.

With my duty done, and a mother to avoid, I headed up to Appletree. During the charcoal-burning heydays this forest was lined with hazel trees, and I was working hard to restore it that way.

These trees like natural light, as shady areas can stunt their growth. They rise from the ground like giant forks, with skinny twigs and leafy bushes. For each hazel stem you cut off, three more will spring up in its place. All this helps to build a strong base.

I stood where I'd caught a glimpse of that girl the other night. Her scent was gone, and only the hot aromas of late June remained.

So I lay in the shade of my hut, listening to some sounds, staring at Cherry's old photo tacked on the wall.

What's that row and rumpus in yer lugs?

I turned off my iPod. 'It's a download, Cherry. Some old mystic hippy type. A bit like yourself.'

Cheeky runt!

'It's my only form of defence.'

Hmm. You been spleening with your mother again?

'She started it. Always does. Now leave me be.' I twiddled the iPod, untangling its white wire.

Where there is no wood, the fire goes out.

I gave up, and lay back on the bed of brushwood. 'You've lost me, Cherry.'

It means that a fiery person causes a quarrel to grow. As charcoal for the embers, and wood for the fire. It makes things flare up.

'Is that your best advice?'

Aye, it is. Heed them words, my lad.

I got up and poked at last night's heap of ashes. Suddenly I raised my hairy head, knowing I was being watched and that someone was close. Seconds later came the cautious tread of a stranger. My heart leaped as I put on Green, Dark & Shady.

But it wasn't the mystery girl with her sweet scent. Like a jungle explorer, a man came swishing through the plant life. His head was bald and rubbery, his neck as thick as a wrestler's. He wore a yellow jacket like a traffic warden, and carried a clipboard.

'Morning,' he grunted, looking around.

'What do you want?'

'Who's asking?'

'The name's Ashburner. I own Appletree Wood.'

The man smiled, as if I'd told him that Santa Claus lived over in Broughton. 'That's dandy,' he said. 'I used to play games in the wood myself.'

'I'm not playing games, you prole. I own the greenery within a good distance of this hut.'

The man's face was as pink as bacon. 'You reckon?'

'I do reckon. And that means you're trespassing.'

'Oh yeah? We'll see about that.'

'See what, slaphead?' But he was already cursing as he moved on through the hazel trees. I threw some cold ashes after him, and they fell to the ground like dead moths.

TEN

'Are you getting a haircut today, Samson?'

'No, Mother. I am not.'

'Then you can't work in the kitchen. You can serve food and clear tables.'

'Whoopee.'

I went out into the lunchtime sunshine. It was a few days since that yellow-coated prat had bungled his way into my woodland, and he'd not been back since.

The paved seating area at the front of The Forge was full. It was on the opposite side of the pub to the car park and kitchen block. We had a party of ten retired plumbers in from Barrow, on a Meal Deal for pensioners. All their chatter was about a new system of toilet piping, recently tried in Kendal. One of them grabbed me as I passed, and pointed at the menu.

'What does this mean, young man? It says here, Eat the View!'

'It means what it says,' I answered. 'Eat the View. We get most of our produce from Wolf Hill farms, and our own orchard and garden.'

His wrinkled face frowned at Mum's daily specials. She went in for local fare made modern:

Risotto of Duddon estuary shrimps
with flat-leaf parsley
and nutmeg;

Peppered medallions of beef
with Madeira and
shallot reduction.

He croaked at me, 'What's the soup?'

'Leek and potato—'

'Ah, very nice.'

'– with Thai flavours.'

'Oh dear.'

The place filled with some right knobs, making sly comments. I pointed at my lugs to show them I could hear.

'That boy waiting on should smile more.'

'Look at his filthy long hair.'

'Why is he wearing dark glasses and a hat?'

At one table, some old drama queen in black was being comforted. She saw me and wailed, 'I have low blood sugar. I need some bread!'

I shuffled off to fetch it but got caught again.

'Excuse me, mate. Did your lambs die a natural death?'

'Eh?'

'Your lamb casserole. How did the animals die? I only eat road kill.'

Mum was in the kitchen dealing with several orders. As I strolled in she snatched a hairnet from a shelf, like the stringy sort that grannies wear in bed.

'Put this on,' she said. 'I need help.'

'Like hell. I'm not going around wearing that.'

'Just do it. Or I'll put it on for you.'

'In that case, I'll be off.'

'To do what?' Mum ranted. 'Lie around in your smelly bed? Or is today set aside for more talking to squirrels?'

'Watch it,' I breathed.

Mum threw the greasy hairnet at me. I threw it back and clenched the handle of a Kitchen Devil. They're well-named, those knives, with blades like the wrath of Satan.

Mum slammed a freezer bag of bilberries on the counter. 'Make a quick sauce with these. Not too much sugar.'

'Bilberries?' I said. 'Where were they nicked from?'

'I picked them near Stephenson Ground. In the hedgerows.'

I couldn't resist. 'Hmm. You realize some fox probably cocked its leg over that lot.'

'Just get on with it.'

'Some fox that had slurped a pool of rabbit pee.'

'I'm not listening.'

'Just imagine the contents of guts like that.'

'No worse, Samson, than the contents of your brain.'

'Or yours, Mother. You sad nutter.'

She screeched at me, arms flailing. 'D'you want the back of my hand?'

My grip tightened on that knife.

'Well, do you, lad? You ready for a thump?'

Kitchen Devil in hand, I charged. 'Yeah?' I yelled. 'You want the back of this?' I stabbed the air by Mum's face. A thrust of cold steel. The blade glinted as she screamed the house down. I nearly took her ear off, swiping the vicious knife about. I stuck it under her fat chin, fingers trembling. Next thing I knew, Dad and one of his mates had my arms gripped.

'Got him,' grunted Dad. I went dead and let myself be marched outside. Dad took the knife from my fist. He drooped with hands on knees, gasping. 'Go, Samson. Get lost and get a grip. We'll manage without.'

I turned and ran into the lane, then fled away downhill.

I stayed at Cherry's hut all afternoon, my anger fuming away inside. 'You're thick, woman!' I shouted back towards The Forge. 'Thick, bloody thick!' I jabbed my head with two fingers, as if ramming a gun into my mother's skull. And the worst of it all was I had no immediate escape in sight. Too scared, and too scarred, for sixth-form college. No chance in the wider world, having messed up at school. My last hope lay in this dark woodland.

I built up a big charcoal stack. It took several hours to burn down, but as it did so that smell of tarry wood began to calm me. The volatiles were slowly being burned off. The smoke was white and dense, like forest fog.

I grabbed some potatoes and veg from a stash crate, to roast in the embers. I wrapped them in foil, laid them on a shovel, and stuck it all into the fiery coals. Dusk fell over the hot evening, and I thought I'd sleep out all night in my clothes. Sitting on an old beer keg, I heard two trees rubbing against each other – a creaky grinding in the stillness.

After I poured water on the stack to cool it, the smoke rose in filthy plumes. Up it went in slow spirals through the clearing above. From the sky it must look like a bald patch in the tree cover.

As I lit the last of my candle lamps, my nose twitched and I sensed another person's presence. I quickly put Green, Dark & Shady back on, then sat and stared at the smoke. The charcoal mound was brooding darkly. Its ashy vapours drifted upward. Then they parted suddenly like curtains being pulled open. And as the clouds cleared, a ghostly shape emerged.

There was a girl on the other side of the pitstead.

She seemed to be standing almost in the coals. Her hair was like a frozen waterfall; almost silver, almost pure white. And she slowly smiled at me.

ELEVEN

I pulled locks of hair over both cheeks, like heavy chains. My face was in shadow, but this girl had no fear of a stranger by his woodland fire. She drifted through the smoke towards me. My lamps had turned the forest into a glowing cave.

The girl wore a black top, with long sleeves and a V-neck. This gave a view of pale skin down to her small breasts. Her blue jeans were cut at the knees. She had a pair of muddy black boots with straggly laces.

As she came closer I saw a ring through her nose. Her hair was dead straight and lay towards her chest. The fringe fell over her right eye.

I sat there spellbound as she stood before me. At last I said, 'Are you for real?'

She kicked me gently. 'Does that feel real?'

I shifted slightly, back into the shadow of Cherry's hut. 'Sure. Thing is, not many girls come this close to me.'

'Maybe you don't go very close to them.'

'Maybe I've good reason not to.'

She stared at me, hardly blinking. I didn't like close scrutiny, especially from such an obvious beauty. 'So, who are you?' I asked. 'What's your name?'

'Angel,' she said. 'Angel Obscura.'

I laughed quietly. 'Sounds more like an email address.'

'It's the name everyone uses for me. What's yours?'

'Samson. Samson Ashburner. My ancestors burned charcoal.'

She perched on a beer crate. 'It's nice. And strange. How old are you?'

'Fifteen, knocking on sixteen. You?'

'The same.'

Her eyes seemed to be all blue, with only a ring of white. They stayed wide open and fixed on me like glass. It made me quite nervy so I pulled my shovel out of the embers. After unwrapping the potatoes and veggies, I said, 'You wanna eat?'

Angel jumped off the crate with joy, like I'd offered her a banquet. She kneeled beside me, blowing on hot spuds and biting their black skins. We scooped cold spring water with our hands from my tin drinking bucket. For a while we sat and just listened as the night owls made mournful echoes. I got a rich scent of perfume like the one I'd sniffed out here a few nights back.

Angel Obscura said, 'Is this where you always hang?'

I nodded, still munching. 'Mostly. My family owns the local pub, but I stay out here. You on holiday?'

She shook her head, biting a blistered asparagus. 'I'm with my parents, but we don't really have holidays.'

'Oh? What do your folks do?'

'We're travellers, so we move about a lot. Squatting places, staying with other travellers, working at fairs. You know.'

I knew nothing about anything except charcoal. 'Uh-huh. So where are you staying right now?'

Angel waved a hand at the dark wood behind. 'Somewhere over there, in a ruined farmhouse. Dad's selling horses at a fair up in Appleby. Then we'll move on.'

My heart caved in, and I hunched against the edge of Cherry's hut. Angel flung a handful of water at me. 'Hey,' she said. 'Why is your face hidden?'

I shrugged and muttered. She crouched before me and stared, as if those eyes were blue oceans to dive through. 'You wanna see something?' she asked.

My heart lit up. See what? Her breasts, her bra, her . . .

'Watch this,' said Angel Obscura. She stood quickly and kicked off her rough boots. She picked up my old shovel, and smoothed the glowing charcoals around the pitstead. They gave out orange flecks, like wild flowers in the gloom. Angel padded to the far side of the mound. She looked keenly at me again, through the threads of smoke. And then she began to walk over the hot coals towards me.

I sat up in shock, but before I could shout she was gliding across. Angel's bare feet hardly seemed to touch the baked blackness. She floated like a phantom, her eyes wide open as if in a trance.

'Are you crazy?' I cried. 'That pit's been burning all day.'

'It's easy, when you know how. Watch.'

And she made a shimmy right back into the cinders. She was even laughing softly to herself, her arms out wide. With quick steps, Angel was over hot ashes and onto the other side. A perfect fire walk. 'You try,' she called across.

'No chance. I grew up in a pub, not a circus.'

'There's no secret,' said Angel. 'You just have to believe.'

This time she came back around the pitstead's edge, and sat on the earth, legs crossed. There was a rip in her jeans near the crotch. My head went thick with desire.

'So,' she said. 'You wanna help me build a home?'

'What sort of home?'

'Well, like a tree house to sleep in. My parents are never very quiet at night. They make out a lot.'

I choked on a hot spud. 'Right,' I said. 'I don't think mine have made out since they made me.'

'That's bad. My last boyfriend was an Irish weaver called Declan. He made these neat clothes from hemp. Y'know hemp, the plant that gives cannabis leaves? Declan was cool, but I'm too young to be tied down.'

'Sure,' I said. 'Always moving on.'

'Yep. We're going to Europe next year, around Scandinavia. I can't wait.' Angel Obscura sprang up. 'So, you'll help me knock together a tree home?'

'OK,' I said. 'I'm often out here.'

'I know. I watched you one night.'

'Yeah. You ran off though.'

Angel stared at me without blinking, then gave me a narrow-eyed look and said, 'I have to go now.'

She lifted her feet and washed them in the tin bucket. I frowned, 'cos that was my pail used for drinking water. It seemed mad to clean her feet and then jam them back into scuzzy old boots.

'D'you know the way?' I said. 'Don't get lost.'

'I walk by moonlight. Every night.'

'Come back soon,' I said. 'Hey, Angel?' But she raced past Cherry's hut, her footsteps rustling into the heart of Appletree Wood. I looked at my watch and it was after midnight.

TWELVE

I doused the last of the charcoals with water, then sat very still. My heart sang from this burst of female closeness, but sank at the thought of Angel seeing me for real. Inside Cherry's hut I fell onto the old sleeping bag over his bushy bed. Moonlight stroked the forest like strobes. A milky ray fell across me, so I lay there like a gleaming figure on his tomb.

My smoky eyes began to feel heavy and I was falling into sleep when a twig cracked somewhere beyond. Footsteps were fumbling my way. For a second I hoped for Angel again, and some wild hint of love in the shadows. But the tread was too heavy for a girl's. A torch flashed on, and shone about like someone searching a dark room.

'Samson? You here, son?'

It was my poor old dad, out in the dead of night.

'I'm here.'

'Ah. There you are. One second.'

'Mind the pitstead,' I said. 'It's still warm.'

Dad tiptoed around the black heap as if it held land mines. I sat on a beer crate as he stood before me looking severe. He leaned over to grab my wrist, and said, 'Never again. Don't ever threaten your mother like that again, or I'll turn on you myself.'

I pulled my hand free, and Dad sat down beside me with a groan. 'Rotten hips,' he said, sounding calmer. 'Years of lugging barrels.'

'Not good.'

'No. Still, it might be the last summer for it. Will be if things don't improve.'

This was scary news for my charcoal plans. 'You're kidding! I know we're pretty remote, and we struggle by . . .'

'We're more than struggling,' said Dad. 'Council tax and rates higher than ever. Less people living in the area all year round, second homes everywhere. And your mum won't drop her standards, so we shell out too much on food. If only I could brew up some decent beers. That'd save us a packet.'

We sat there in quiet thought as trees huddled around in gloomy gangs. At last Dad said, 'And your mother's not so well, with all the worry. Can't have the two of you fighting like cat and dog all summer. Another scene like today might finish me.'

I stroked the hidden redness on my face. And I thought, there are scars deep inside you that time might heal, but the ones on the outside could never fade.

Dad read my mind. 'Do you still think what happened was your mother's fault? I mean, it's five years back. Nearly six now.'

'I know,' I said. 'She bullied me into going that day. That's all I remember.'

It wasn't all I could remember. I could recall her years of coldness, and her lack of tender concern. All her bustling about and shouting in the kitchen was like something to hide behind, so she never had to stop and be a mother. Maybe she wasn't much of a wife either.

Dad held out a package. 'Your mum sent you something. Home-made foccaccia, with onions and cheddar. Go on, you love this.'

I did love it, but I wouldn't take the peace offering. Dad sighed deeply and took a bite himself. 'Just try and meet her halfway, son. If we can see this summer through, there's a chance of some daylight. If not, we could be sold up and gone by Christmas. Do you want that?'

'No. I like being here in my wood.'

'Aye,' said Dad, 'that's another thing. You've turned into a right hermit. What about sixth-form college in September? That course in Barrow does customer service and chef skills.'

I got to my feet, brushing myself. 'I'm done with schools.'

'What'll you do instead?'

'I've a plan for my charcoal. Give me time.'

Dad turned on his torch, and stood stiffly. 'Time's running out, Sam. We're nearly at crisis point. Come home, please.'

I led us back out of Appletree Wood, holding aside

branches from Dad's face. We plodded up the lane in dead summer silence. As we approached The Forge, my father said, 'Can you hold the fort tomorrow? Your mother's got a hospital appointment and I'm taking her in.'

'I guess. Can't see it being busy.'

'Good forecast,' said Dad, scanning the clouds. 'Be better for us if it rained, and everyone came inland. Night then, son. And remember what I said.'

'Night.'

I wasn't ready for sleep yet. I wanted to sit on the swings and murmur Angel Obscura's name. To close my eyes and see her fragile vision come through the charcoal smoke again. I crunched over the car park to the kiddie zone. A grove of fruit trees made a border around the grassy clearing.

The games and amusements looked spooky by moonlight. A seesaw lay at rest, with one end pointing to the stars. A small roundabout glowed white. Each of its seats had a painted clown's face. When I pushed the thing around it gave a squeak.

The wooden climbing frame was like a toy castle. A skull and cross-bones flag hung limply from its central pole. And for the sandpit, Mum drove ten miles to Silecroft every summer to get fresh sand from the beach there.

I sat on a swing and rocked gently. The trees of our ancient orchard stood watching, many of them bearing rare fruits. A weirdy beardy man from the Pear

Association came one time, to take grafts of our unusual species. He took a liking to The Forge with its well-kept beers, but he got so drunk he had to stay in our spare room, where he also wet the camp bed that night.

As I swung and dreamed, I heard voices from the lane to my left. Two men were in conversation, not aware that anyone was listening. They walked slowly downhill in the deep shade of hedgerows. I sat in silence and listened hard. The first guy had a posh accent. He said, 'Oh, Gregson? One other thing. Can we get the heavy machinery down this lane?'

The second voice was rougher, more local. I recognized it straight off. 'I think so, Lord Standish. And there's a bridleway leading up to the wood. A bit narrow, like, but OK for my earth mover.'

'Good, good. A prime site is Ashburner's Wood.'

'Appletree Wood, sir.'

'Yes, of course. I keep seeing its original name on my old plans. It's rather stuck with me.'

Quiet as a shadow, I eased myself off the swing. The garden was ringed with fruit trees, and I pressed myself against one to hear more.

Standish spoke in a clear, cut-glass tone. 'How soon can you prepare the ground?'

'Tomorrow morning, sir,' answered the other. 'First thing.'

'OK. The sooner the better, Gregson. Before any voices are raised against us.'

The conversation trailed away, as the two men sauntered down towards the old ivy cottage. I got a whiff of cigar smoke in the still night air. But by the time I crept out into the lane, there was only a rustle of wild creatures and the dark of thick shrubs.

THIRTEEN

I slept badly in a sweat of deep anxiety. It must have been Lord Hugo Standish talking last night, and that Gregson bloke must be the meathead who'd invaded my wood recently.

I got up and pulled on my I'M A LIVING APE-MAN T-shirt. I rated it as Mum's third least favourite of mine. The early morning was quiet, except for the cock-a-doodle cry of a rooster on the farm behind Harker Hall, where I was headed.

A steel farm gate leading onto Harker's driveway was closed. On the grass verge beyond it lay a pair of kiddie bikes – for the twins I'd seen with Lady Standish. The square grey house looked unlived in, its private buildings around the back lost among trees.

That rooster crowed again on full throttle, and as it squawked I heard the thud of a window slamming. I grinned, and thought of the Standish set trying to sleep through this rustic racket.

I was about to hop over the gate and snoop around, when something came clattering along the narrow road into Wolf Hill. I took cover among bushes as a yellow earth mover went snorting by. It had a huge scooper at the front which bounced on the tarmac. I sneaked out from my hiding place and watched it plough along, until it reached the old ivy cottage. Then the earth mover made a right turn, where the lane grew narrow and formed a bridleway. It just squeezed onto it, and drove on, scraping fences and hedges.

I ran over the road to a drystone wall, topped with barbed wire. To my left, I watched the machine as it pushed up the bridleway towards Appletree. I gripped between the wire's barbs, anxious to see if my fears were true.

There was no way the earth machine could get much further. Where the bridleway ended was the entrance to my wood on the right. The trees there began to cluster, and a path led towards Charcoal Cherry's hut. But the great vehicle went on as if nothing stood before it. A mashing of bracken and twigs arose from Appletree Wood like an army on the rampage.

At that point I slipped over the wall, snagging my jeans on wire. I crept slowly through the sleepy meadows, then ran full pelt through the barley field beyond. The earth mover stopped suddenly and peace returned to Wolf Hill, the sky already bright with fresh clouds, and nothing made a sound except for that rooster. I felt in the grip of some insane dream and made my way to the lowest edge of Appletree. All animal noise had ceased after the motorized invasion – even the distant rooster was muted – and I knew roughly where the machine must be parked.

I forced myself to make a move. 'Who's up there?' I shouted, shoving pine branches. 'What are you doing?'

No one answered my angry huffing, but soon I got a glimpse of yellow-brown metal through the greenery. I hacked a route through, and wailed at the destruction.

Bright green ferns had been trampled. The heads of wild flowers lay crumpled. And several of my precious hazel trees for charcoal burning had been flattened.

There was no sign of the earth mover's driver. The cabin door was closed, and climbing up to open it I found it locked. By the pedals was a girly magazine, open at the picture of some naked babe. Even in such a rage I twisted my head for a closer look.

'Who's out here?' I shouted. 'Where are you?' I thumped the metal doors. In protest, I jumped down and sat inside the great front shovel, which was caked with dried mud, its teeth blunt with endless digging. But still nobody came back as time dragged on in the humid wood. Birdsong returned, a new day revved into life at Wolf Hill's farms, and that rooster beyond Harker began blowing its rusty trumpet again.

It was about an hour later when footsteps finally came towards me, from the direction of Cherry's hut. I waited for Gregson to appear, and maybe a bunch of his cronies.

Then came a tingling voice. 'Samson? Samson Ashburner?' It was Angel Obscura.

'Over here!' I shouted.

Angel stumbled through the shrubs and stood

before me. Her platinum-blonde hair fell in a path to her breasts. Her eyes were blue crystals. Her pale face had hardly a speck of colour. She wore a white dress with long sleeves, and those grungy boots again. I felt gruesome in Green, Dark & Shady; my hair was all skanky.

'Hey there,' I said, shrinking into the shade.

'Hey,' said Angel. 'What's that dumper doing here?'

'Mashing up my woodland. Some local big shot sent it.'

'Rich scum,' said Angel. 'So, is this forest really yours?'

'Yep. It's in a contract that my great-grandpa and Lord Harker once drew up. It says that after Cherry's death this patch of woodland is handed down to the youngest child of the family. There's a clause about supplying cherry brandy to the Harkers. But the home brews died out with Cherry, at least until my dad's manky efforts.'

Angel stood in a patch of sunlit bracken. 'Wait here,' she said, and ran back towards the pitstead.

A few minutes later she returned with my bill-hook. She hit the earth mover's giant shovel in protest, then prised open the engine casing with its sharp edge. Raising my billhook on high, she slashed it down inside. A wire snapped and spat back. Something metallic pinged off into the grass. I heard liquid dribbling, like a water can had been tipped.

I gripped my long hair in shock. 'What you doing? That's enough!'

But it wasn't. Angel's face was hard with rage as she did a real hatchet job on that machine. She jabbed my billhook into the tyres, time and again. Each thick rubbery tread gave way to her fury as splits appeared in them. For such a frail girl she found wild strength, attacking the digger like it had done her a great wrong.

Finally I had to wrestle the billhook away. 'Enough,' I said. 'There's other ways.' I held her arms as she slowly calmed down. She trembled like a trapped animal. 'It's OK,' I said. 'I wanna do the same. But we'd better shoot. They'll think it was me did this.'

'But it wasn't you,' said Angel, quieter now. She pushed me away. 'Let's go then. There's a place I wanna take you. We can hang out there all day.'

Fourteen

Angel took me beyond Cherry's wigwam hut and its ashy pitstead. I kept looking back in case Gregson, or whoever, returned for that earth mover.

We pressed on to where Appletree Wood grew dense with dark pines. The gloom there suited me well as my face was less obvious, but Angel walked beyond this until we met a giant dawn redwood tree. Two hundred years back, a retired ship's captain planted seeds here with trees from every country he'd visited. This dawn redwood was one of them. It stood out like a towering landmark, so its ironic local nickname was Red Dwarf.

'Up there for my tree house,' said Angel.

My neck creaked back at this wooden stairway to the stars.

'You sure? It's a protected species.'

'This one,' said Angel firmly. 'I wanna go really high. Out of everyone's reach.'

Dawn redwoods have a muscular red-brown trunk. In autumn their leaves are a vivid orange, and in summer they turn glossy green.

Appletree was a real English woodland, like a tree museum. But further along was the Forestry Commission's private land, where they grew acres of regular conifers. Each tree in there was like a dumb brown pole. The side branches were trimmed when they were ready to be harvested, and the trunks put through a saw mill. Out of this came lots of ready-made planks, like the forest was just a wood factory.

'Ready?' said Angel. 'Let's climb.'

Before I could answer, she was onto the reddish bark like a koala. She inched up to the lower branches, her short dress lifting. I stood right below her staring at the sweet bliss on display. My brain melted with every flash of white knickers. When she was perched safely, she said, 'Come on!'

My arms and chest were toned through years of cutting branches, and I easily hauled my bones up to Angel. When my monkish hood fell back, I covered my head again.

'Hey,' she said. 'You needn't hide from me.'

'I'm not hiding,' I mumbled, then changed the subject. 'I think these branches are strong enough.'

Angel bounced on her bum. 'Yeah. I'm not building a mansion. Don't need a fancy kitchen.'

'Right,' I said. 'Oh, hellfire! Kitchens. What's the time?'

Angel checked her watch. 'Nearly eleven.'

'I should be at work.' I began to slither down. My parents must have been waiting ages for me. 'Gotta run.'

'Don't go,' called Angel. 'Stay here with me.'

It was like the tempting song of a sea siren, but I ignored it and bombed through the bushes. Minutes later I was lurching into The Forge's car park, where a few vehicles were standing. Mum and Dad were going nuts by the kitchen block, our car doors wide open.

'Samson!' Dad shouted. 'We're late for your mother's appointment. Get into the kitchen and start prepping. Now!'

Mum went gasping to the car, really hamming it up like she was dying of black lung disease. She wobbled on elephant legs, shouting at me about Cumbria pancetta, a rack of lamb, and what a waste of space I was.

I stormed into the kitchen, feeling evil. I was deprived of a day with Angel, and I was also losing control of my woodland. Somebody out there was messing with my heritage.

One of Dad's mates ran the bar, leaving me in charge of the kitchen. In truth, I did enjoy cooking and tarting around with food, but as it was my mother's great passion I made out it was a drag.

Most of the prep work had been done so I fluffed up the salads and made some fresh dressings. The daily special was roast rack of Cumbrian lamb, using the meat of young sheep from Wilson's farm. We also did cheesy ciabattas, chips and such stuff at lunchtime – which was what most people went for – but Mum couldn't resist the posher items for her specials. Dad was always moaning about her pricey ingredients, even if most of it did come from local farms. 'Eat the View' was Mum's motto, and she stuck to it.

After I'd prepared each meal, I put on Green, Dark & Shady and pulled my hair across. Then it was away with a tray of dishes to the tables outside, where a few people sweltered under a blistering sun. The customers looked at me in alarm, as if I might pull a knife. 'Bon appy tits,' I said, slamming down the plates.

I hurried back indoors, desperate to head to Appletree. But then Dad phoned and he sounded well hacked off. 'Samson. They want to do more tests. You'll have to prepare the evening menu.'

'You're kidding.'

'I'm not. And I'm still angry with you for being late. I thought we had an agreement after last night.'

'Yeah, well. Things have happened since then.'

'What things?'

'Bad things in my wood.'

'I can't talk now. The menus are on the computer. OK?'

'OK,' I sighed.

'I'll give Mum your love. Don't let us down.'

He rang off without waiting for a reply. I hopped around, and kept running into the narrow road to listen for earth-moving activity. But it seemed like Angel had spiked that machine's motor and tyres really well. As I was heading back to the kitchen, someone clicked their fingers behind me. I turned and saw an elegant man there, holding one of The Forge's flyers. He was maybe my dad's age, but his light blue suit and styled fair hair were immaculate. His jawbone was rock hard. He took off a pair of film-star sunglasses and regarded me.

'Samson Ashburner?'

'Might be,' I grunted, wiping my nose.

'I am Lord Hugo Standish, of Harker Hall. I wish to speak with your parents.'

Fifteen

Even though my face was hidden I knew it had gone white. Sweat trickled down my neck like a slug's gloop. This guy before me oozed class and money. Was he here to drag me away for battering an earth mover?

'Uh. Well, they're not home,' I said. 'Can I help?'

Lord Standish showed me the pub flyer. 'You gave this to my wife recently. But it doesn't mention whether you do accommodation here.'

Blood flowed back to my face. 'Ah, yeah. No, we don't. There's only space for three of us.'

His lordship pocketed the brochure. 'A shame,' he said. 'I need rooms for my workmen, and Harker Hall's outbuildings aren't enough.'

'Workmen doing what?'

He crumpled the flyer. 'Important work for the local area. This little pub might yet feel the benefits of it. I see your business is not exactly booming.'

You could hear generations of smug money talking.

'Well, you gather wrong,' I said. 'Some of us care about quality, not a fast buck. And what new project are you setting up around here?'

Lord Standish put his sunglasses back on. 'Careful,' he

said softly. 'Never punch over your weight. Or get ideas above your station.' And with that he started down the lane, a mobile buzzing in his pocket. He stood in the shade of high hedges and answered it. 'What? Damaged where? The tyres slashed?'

I leaped back into the safety of our kitchen among dried hams and gingerbread. I even closed the door, despite the heat, and bolted it. For now I was happy to stay in The Forge, out of harm's way.

'Not that you bothered to ask,' said Dad, 'but your mother is going back to hospital next week for more tests.'

I was washing up in the kitchen after the evening meal service. Mum had gone upstairs to lie down, on Dad's orders. He tried again. 'I said, your mother is going—'

'I heard you. What can I do? I'm not a doctor.'

'You could show a little sympathy. She can hardly breathe some days.'

'Bad pollen vibes,' I said. 'Long hot summer.'

Dad started stacking the clean dishes. 'It might help her if you had some focus, Sam. A bit of interest in doing catering at sixth-form college, maybe? You could get buses to Barrow and back each day.'

I felt a mix of anger and anxiety. It welled up until I bashed a row of dishes. Dad jumped away and dropped a plate.

I stumbled to the kitchen table, slumped forward in a chair, and rested my forehead on the wooden surface. I wrapped both arms around my head. Dad came close and gently rubbed my back. 'What is it, Samson? What scares you so much?'

He pulled up a chair as my tears found a way through the dam I'd been building for years. The drops ran down, tickling my chin. Dad sat there patiently, easing my neck with a soft hand. 'Can't you tell me? Is it private?'

I shook my head, wiping away salty dribbles. 'It's just . . . It's just that I can't face a new load of strangers. It's the girls mostly, how they stare when they see all this.' I pointed at my face.

Dad sighed with disappointment. 'I'm so sorry,' he said. 'I thought maybe you'd learned to live with it.'

'You never learn to live with it. Why d'you think I like burning charcoal? It takes me out there on my own, and my face gets good and filthy.'

A few drunken voices came through the wall from the front bar. The same few locals I'd heard for most of my life. The kitchen door was open with all the sweet ache of a summer night beyond it. Somewhere out there, people my age were cutting loose and loving wildly.

Dad looked shattered. He rubbed his curly brown hair, his belly heaving. 'Honest, Sam, it's not as bad as you think. I mean, I hardly even notice it now.'

I laughed and sobbed. 'Cheers, Dad. But you're not everyone. And sixth-form won't happen 'cos I failed all my exams. On purpose.'

This brought a great groan from Dad that silenced the front bar. Someone shouted, 'You all right, Peter? What's the missus doing?'

More evil cackles came from the regulars. Dad said, 'That's not good, son. Your mother's gonna blow. We're over ten thousand pounds in debt right now, and our worries are piling high.'

I stood up. 'I can pay my way with charcoal, even more so if my business plan kicks off. Look, I need some air. Been cooped up here all day.'

'Aye, I know. We'll talk another time.'

Up in Appletree Wood, that abandoned earth mover loomed like a dinosaur, its engine closed and sealed, its tyres ruined. Deeper into the dark forest I found white spray paint on various trees. They were being marked out for some purpose.

But another thing was bothering me. The wood was too quiet. It felt like the end of all time. Like a world without animal or human noise. Not a note of birdsong came from the branches. Not even a grey squirrel scratched on tree bark. I knew then that I wasn't alone. Something, or somebody, was nearby. I could feel them like a cold shadow.

'Angel?' I breathed. The space between each tree seemed filled with phantoms.

'Anyone!' I shouted. 'Show yourself.'

Like a rushing wind, somebody burst from the trees behind me. I was knocked flat to the forest floor. Heavy hands pressed my nose into the dirt. Gregson's voice hissed, 'Keep your hands off people's property.'

As my attacker barged away, I looked up to see the stocky thug hustle through the trees. Tall and tough as I'd grown, I was no match for this heavy. I let him disappear.

SIXTEEN

Next morning after breakfast I went storming down to Harker Hall.

Not only had Lord Standish insulted me – in my own backyard. But one of his muscled bullies had roughed me up – in my own forest. I pulled on Green, Dark & Shady, throwing my face into shadow.

Nobody answered when I hammered the door. I cupped my hands to peer through a window, ablaze with sunshine. That's when Lady Standish opened the door, wearing a peach dress suit. She had that sorrowful stare again, with a silver-blue glint on her perfect cheekbones. I imagined her gazing into a cold fireplace for hours.

'I'm just taking the twins out,' she said. 'Did you wish to see me?'

'Huh? Oh, no, it was your husband. He's messing about on my land.'

'Is he, indeed? And what land is that?'

'Appletree Wood,' I said. 'It's mine by ancient deed.'

Lady Standish placed a hand on either side of hourglass hips. She twirled a thread of bleached blonde hair. 'I will be sure to tell him. And I don't suppose you can throttle that miserable cockerel?'

The rooster was still bellowing, like it wanted daybreak to party on for ever. 'Uh, no. You'll get used to it.'

'I doubt that. The farmer refuses to keep his noisy bird indoors, so I intend taking out a court order.'

'Against the farmer?'

'Against the rooster,' said Lady Standish. The perfect mask of her face never slipped. 'You have an interesting style,' she said to me. 'This dark and dangerous uniform you wear. Do you model?'

I gasped and laughed. 'Do I heck! Why?'

She couldn't resist checking her reflection in the window. 'The agencies go for all types,' she said. 'I've worked for one of them.'

'Yeah? Cool.'

The golden twins came outside, howling with boredom. Lady Standish observed me closely, then pulled the door to. 'I'll inform my husband of your claims,' she said, and swayed gracefully over to the Mercedes.

Next day, Angel Obscura lay giggling on the forest floor. 'You mean, she's taking a rooster to court? Tasteless toff.'

'It's not funny,' I said, raking the ashes around my pitstead. 'Lord Standing Joke even said his workmen are moving in here. But they can't do anything without my permission. And I wouldn't let them.'

'No?' said Angel. She drew her boots towards her bum, parting her knees. I saw right up her grubby white dress. 'Not for, say, five grand?'

'Make it five million and the answer's still no.'

'Cool. My dad's real brainy, but like you he'd never sell his soul to the business world.'

'That's good,' I said. 'I'd like to meet your parents.'

'I've told them about you. And I've made a start on my tree house. You wanna see?'

The great dawn redwood glowed under streams of sunshine. Looking up, I could just see planks and ferns in a heap. Angel said, 'I've got some tools from my dad. Give me a hand?'

I'd built up my own woodland hideout over the years, so this tree house was gonna be a doddle. 'Sure, Angel. Lead on.'

She shinned her way up the redwood, having hacked some footholds into the protected tree's bark. The higher we climbed, the thicker the branches grew in a close web. At about ten metres from ground level, they stuck out like a series of cross beams. This was where Angel had chosen to site her den. There was a bottle of water and some biscuits.

'Just enough space to crash,' she said. 'Or to come and chill.'

It must have taken several climbs for her to get the old planks up there. I hammered away at them until a bed-shaped platform was in place. Angel tied some cut bracken around it and stacked leafy ferns above the tiny stage. 'Should keep the rain off,' she said.

'Rain!' I laughed. 'You'll not see much rain before September.'

'We won't be here in September. We'll have a new caravan that we're doing up. Then it's back on the road.'

Before I could groan about her leaving, we heard someone trampling below. I parted the leaves and looked down. 'It's Standish,' I whispered. 'The toss from Harker Hall.'

We hid among the branches and bracken. Standish's voice was cold, like a foggy cloud in winter, as he paced around with mobile in hand. 'We'll need to bulldoze the trees in that top corner,' he said. 'Those tall thin ones.'

'My hazels!' I gasped. Angel put a hand over my lips.

Standish went on. 'I need a basic road putting through. Once we've got something up and running, it's harder for anyone to raise objections.' He jabbed out his cigar on a sycamore, crushing it into the trunk like he meant to torture it.

'No, no,' he continued. 'It's not even a village here. Just a bunch of hayseed farmers and a pub straight out of Dickens. Could make a decent wine bar of it.'

I nearly fell off the nailed planks. Angel stared at me from that white face, her blue eyes like hard pebbles.

Standish pulled out his wallet and found a card. 'Let me give you Carlo's number in London,' he said, and read out some digits. 'Any expenses over five grand can go through him.'

A minute later he rang off, and strode away until the wood covered his trail. When I turned back to Angel, she was scratching herself madly on both arms. She breathed quickly, her eyes glazed over as if she was drugged. Her nails raked ever harder.

'Hey, careful,' I said. 'Did something sting you?'

She slowed up, and began to breathe more evenly. 'It's OK,' she said. 'People like that make me dead itchy. It's like I wanna peel off all my skin.'

'I'm going down after him. I want some answers.'

Angel laid a hand on mine. 'Stay here, Samson. Just for a bit. I want you to take off all this heavy gear. I want to see the real you.'

SEVENTEEN

With shaky hands I reached for Angel's bottle of water. 'Um, what d'you mean by all this heavy gear?'

Angel crossed her legs. Bronze light lay upon her limbs. 'This cap,' she said, touching my head. 'This hood, this hair, these glasses. Show me what's under it all.'

And so . . . I decided to tell her the story of that birthday party at Wilson's farm. I told her of the isolation I had always felt, and of the distance it put between me and girls like her. 'Except you're not like other girls,' I said. 'You don't junk me.'

Angel shrugged her bony shoulders. 'Living on the road we don't judge people by their looks. I've worked at circuses and such like with real freaks. You're just a lonely boy who's never known how special he is.'

That made me blush. Angel Obscura lay down beside me, her head on a pillow of forest greenery. Like a dreamer, I reached out nervously to touch the damp skin below her neck.

'Not now,' she whispered. 'Not yet.'

'No,' I mumbled. 'Sorry. Look, can I save the big reveal for another time?'

'Sure. I wasn't pushing you. And listen, you've

helped me with this tree house, so what can I do for you?'

I laughed and cracked a joke. 'You can break into Harker Hall. Find out what Standish is planning.'

Angel curled up like a cat, her white dress all scrunched. She stared at me without blinking, then said, 'You can meet my parents tomorrow. They're chilling at the squat for a few days.'

'Heck, yeah,' I said. 'I'd love to meet some real people. Right now, I'm late for work. Come and find me tomorrow.' I was lit by a sudden joy at Angel's invite, and leaped from the tree's lowest branch like a bushman. Running home, I stopped by that earth mover and spat a great gob down its windscreen.

Early next morning, Dad decided that Mum and me should go on a bonding mission, to promote The Forge in nearby Coniston.

I sat in the car with a box of pub flyers, edging away from my mother against the door. Tourist vehicles jammed the roads, many with canoes tightly strapped on their bonnets, while others towed large motor boats. All were heading for Coniston Water, or further on towards the great lake at Windermere.

Every hill and moorland lay awash with purple. It was like the landscape had been soaked in wine. Gorse bushes pushed their yellow flowers to the sun.

'Beautiful,' said Mum. She was speaking more to herself than me.

'Huh? Hmm.' For me there was beauty enough to protect in Appletree Wood, and some of this area could go figure. Most of it gleamed like pages from a tourist brochure. I'd rather get down and dirty among charcoal fires.

The road was rammed on the way into Coniston, as 4x4s and Range Rovers barged through like tanks. Cars were queuing six deep into the garage for petrol. Every pub's outdoor area was filling up, and people strolled the pavements licking ice creams. Kids from my school year served in the cafés and tea rooms. Through a window I saw two of them edging past each other with heavy trays. I looked away, and there, rising above everything were the sun-bronzed mountains. They watched over this crazy scheme of things like silent gods.

After waiting for fifteen minutes, my mother found a parking space behind the tourist office in the village centre. She got out on slabby feet and shuffled off. 'Come on. Bring that box of brochures.'

I threw on Green, Dark & Shady, and with a quick glance in the wing mirror I fixed my hair across the gaps.

My mother sighed. 'You look like a mugger.'

We knocked on various doors along a row of council homes. One was opened by an unshaven brute, with whisky breath and home-made tattoos. He said, 'Get shot, or I'll set my dogs on you.' Other people were nicer, took a flyer, and wished us well.

But over on the posher estate it was hopeless, because so few of the big houses there were being lived in. A frail old lady opened the door at one. 'I'm only the housekeeper,' she said. 'The owners are coming here in August, for a fortnight. No more than that. They pay me to keep the dust off.'

It was the same story elsewhere. Another local housekeeper came to the door, her roll-up ciggy like a hag's finger. 'You've just missed them,' she croaked at me. 'They're not back now until Christmas.'

She watched her fag ash drop to the floor. 'That's how some folks live,' she went on. 'I can't think why they come here at all. You look up there it's the bloomin' hills, down there it's the bleedin' lake.'

Mum caught me up and grabbed my elbow. 'Let's go,' she said. 'There's nothing much for us here.'

That evening, we held a council of war in the pub's kitchen. Dad laid out our bank statements and accounts. 'We're nearly eleven grand in debt,' he said. 'Some of that's tied up in stock and assets, but it's still a hefty wedge. Unless trade really booms over the rest of the summer, we'll have to sell up. So then, who's got any big ideas?'

I shuffled my boots under the table. 'We're not doing anything wrong. We just never get much passing trade, stuck out on a limb like this.'

Mum said, 'We should make more of the crowds on the main road to Coniston. Get some of them coming here.'

'Aye,' said Dad. 'There's the annual Lake Race soon. We could muscle in.'

'Exactly,' said Mum. 'You could get a big sign made up. Samson can go and stand by the roadside with it as the runners go by.'

'Cheers, Mum. Mong in the sun all day and be gawped at.'

'Samson!' My mother slapped the table. 'Unless you've got the odd ten grand stashed away, you'll do your bit. And get your bloody hair cut.'

I shoved the table and stormed out. I had a woodland of rare hazel trees to protect, and an earth mover sat among them like a ticking bomb.

In the warm twilight that evening it was still there. I wrote DEATH TO DESTROYERS in the dirt along one side, then went to find comfort in Cherry's old wigwam. I took out some dried hazel branches, and cut them into small lengths with my billhook. I brushed away old ashes from the pitstead, and smeared my face with charcoal bits, sifting out the best lumps from a recent batch.

Then I sat among the trees and listened to nature. I closed my eyes and heard the rapid call of a nightjar. It was perched along a dead branch somewhere behind me. The sound was like a little motor revving up.

Churrrrr . . . Jarrrrr . . . Churrrr . . . Jarrrrrrr . . .

I knew there'd be no chance of spotting the bird, 'cos its grey-brown plumage was a perfect forest camouflage.

Churrrrr . . . Jarrrrr . . . Churrrr . . . Jarrrrrrr . . .

On it went without a break for minutes at a time. Then suddenly the nightjar shut up as if its engine had been switched off. I opened my eyes, wondering what had caused it to hush. A few seconds later, something came bashing through the trees behind the hut. It wasn't a deer – they moved carefully and quietly. This was a human chaos and it sounded desperate. I stood up, my heart knocking, as somebody crashed their way ever closer. A frail white figure rushed at me like a ghost. It was Angel Obscura with a fistful of papers.

'Samson!' She grabbed my hand, pulling me along. 'Quick, quick,' she begged. 'They're chasing me.'

My brain swirled as I led her away at speed. We stumbled and ran but Angel kept looking behind her. 'What is it?' I said, gasping. 'Who's coming?'

'Just keep going! Where can we hide?'

Eighteen

I dragged Angel up to the top ridge of my wood. From there the landscape climbed in little hills towards Stickle Pike. Crumbling drystone walls lined the way, and in the gathering dark we could lose ourselves among them. The fells were thick with dark green bracken.

We lurched our way up to the high ground. At no time did I hear anyone giving chase but my blood was pounding in both ears. At last I pushed Angel down beside a high wall in the shadows of a mound. We lay and panted like hunted creatures.

Angel was breathless and her nose was running. When at last I could speak, I said, 'What the hell happened?'

Angel held out the papers she was carrying. 'I did it,' she gasped. 'Like you asked. I broke into Harker Hall and stole this stuff, then someone came chasing after me.'

I stared at her in shock. 'What? I can't believe you broke in. I never really meant that.'

Angel thrust a big sheet at me. It looked like the planned version of a magazine advert. The main part of it showed a photograph of Appletree Wood taken from the air. You could see my ridge of forest, between Wilson's farm on the left, and the Forestry Commission land on the right.

Several white arrows had been inked across the view, pointing right into Appletree. One of them would be almost over Cherry's hut. And in thin white writing were the words, YOUR HOUSE GOES HERE! Parts of the picture had been airbrushed, so you could see how the wood might look with loads of trees taken out. I was shaking like a loon as I read the bold details below.

- **Three-bedroom luxury log cabins, in quiet Lakeland hamlet**

- **New community in remote farming region**

- **Attractive long-term investment**

- **Ideal as a second home or holiday let**

- **Free use of local helipad**

I grabbed another document, with several phrases highlighted in pink pen.

'WOLF HILL SITE . . . Plots of up to one acre . . . From £300,000 . . . Prices subject to currency fluctuation . . . All contracts take place in UK sterling . . . 20% reduction for early buyers . . .'

'Are these the only copies?' I asked.

'No,' said Angel. 'I just took things that had duplicates.'

I crunched the papers. 'I'll petrol bomb Harker Hall.'

'Let's do it,' said Angel. 'We were travelling down in Cornwall last summer, and this group called the Cornish Liberation Army set fire to a holiday home. Then we all moved in and squatted it.'

I didn't know about Cornwall, but I knew my woodland was a sacred site, it was mine by birthright, and I had nowhere else to hide.

Angel breathed at me, 'What you thinking?'

'I'm thinking it's time to strike back,' I said. 'Maybe I can talk to your folks about this tomorrow. Get some ideas from two real rebels.'

Angel said something about the Cornish Army again, but her voice was drowned by the sudden clatter of a helicopter. It soared above us like a mythical beast, its blades whirling. I read, MOUNTAIN RESCUE, painted along one side.

'That'll be from Coniston,' I said. 'Maybe someone's bust a leg on Dow Crag.'

'People don't climb mountains at night,' said Angel.

'They do on holiday. They go bloody mad on holiday.'

The helicopter soared off into the sunset. Angel peeped above the drystone wall back towards Appletree.

'No one followed us,' she said. 'But they might be waiting somewhere.'

'So who was chasing you? Lord Standish?'

'Doubt it. Be one of his sidekicks. I think they gave up when I hit the wood.'

'You gave me a right start,' I said. 'Still, I'm chuffed you got your hands on this stuff. Where was it?'

Angel sat back against the wall. 'There's an office around the back of Harker. The window was open, so I went in. I could hear the lord and lady having a barney about something.'

'Then what?'

'I had a quick root around, grabbed these papers and ran. When I cut across the fields I heard some bloke shouting. His voice got closer but I never looked back.'

'You're amazing,' I said. I risked a peek over the wall, as if expecting a bullet to zap me. 'Come on. We'll take the path behind Appletree, down that big slope of moorland. I'll see you home.'

'No need,' said Angel. She got up and climbed over the wall. 'Meet me about three tomorrow at my tree house.' And she was away like a mountain goat, skipping over stones and down hillocks. Her trim white figure was soon lost among the shadows of the fells.

I sat back in deep thought, under the first coolness of night. By the time I ambled home I had the stirrings of a plan, inspired by something Angel had said.

Dad was tidying the pub as I slipped upstairs into our

little spare room where the computer was kept. The desk was crowded with files, bills and invoices.

I sat down and typed the first draft of a letter. I felt moved to do something and this is what I wrote.

```
LET IT BE HEARD. THE PEOPLE'S
ARMY OF CUMBRIA DEMANDS AN END
TO THE INVASION OF OUR REGION.
ALL RICH INCOMERS, AND HOLIDAY-
HOME OWNERS, WILL BE DRIVEN OUT.
    WE ARE MORE THAN A HUNDRED
PEOPLE STRONG, UNABLE TO AFFORD
HOMES IN THE COUNTY OF OUR
BIRTH. WE INTEND TO FIGHT TO
PROTECT OUR HERITAGE.
    ANY NEW HOLIDAY HOMES WILL BE
TORCHED.
                THE CUMBRIAN PHOENIX
```

Nineteen

Early next morning, 'the Cumbrian Phoenix' walked up the lane out of Wolf Hill. I carried an envelope addressed to the local *Evening Post*, written in a spidery disguise. At the top, I shoved it into the red letterbox. If it got printed in the paper I could slide a copy through Standish's door, to make his lordship take notice and give him second thoughts.

I crossed the quiet lane above Wolf Hill, and looked down the fields to the main road far below. It was filled with cars en route from Broughton to Coniston. They crawled nose to tail, like some endless metal crocodile. Many were heading into Coniston for the annual Lake Race, which I hoped my parents had forgotten about.

But no such luck. Back at The Forge, my dad was busy by his workshed. He put out the pub's signboard, with his new chalked slogan for the day.

WELCOME TO THE FORGE AT WOLF HILL

NO HOOLIGANS!

NO HOBBITS!

And to my dismay, he'd been working on a new and bigger panel. It was over a metre square, with carefully painted lettering.

THE FORGE AT WOLF HILL
GOOD BEER GUIDE & AA RECOMMENDED
OFF THE TORVER TO BROUGHTON ROAD
TALLY HO!

'Must you put "Tally Ho"?' I asked. 'We'll get the hunting-shooting crowd.'

'Samson,' gasped Dad, lugging the sign to the car, 'right now I'd take the Swingers of Satan crowd if they had money to spend. You ready? We're leaving in five minutes.'

Mum shouted from the kitchen window. 'And leave your hat, hood and dark glasses here. Or you'll scare everyone away.'

Quarter of an hour later I was beside a lay-by on the Coniston road, with bottled water, sandwiches and my iPod. I sat behind the stupid board as the sun beat down like a blacksmith's hammer. Every car that went past was filled with tracksuiters, ready to hoof it around Coniston Water.

I turned the iPod up to drown out each whooshing car. Cosmic pulses and dubby beats throbbed in my ears. Soon enough, the race officials came cycling by to take their positions.

'Break your legs,' I muttered.

The first runners appeared on my right like a fleeing army. They pounded the sizzling tarmac in white shirts with numbered bibs. Some of the dumb athletic types from school were in among them too. I turned the trance music even higher.

Maybe everyone looked at our pub sign as they went by. It was a moment of novelty in the humdrum of a long hot race, where thousands of bodies plodded along.

I had a call from my dad just after two o'clock, when I was starting to get het up about seeing Angel at three. It would be wild to meet her parents.

'Dad. Where are you?'

'Sorry, we've been busy. Seems like the plan worked today, so well done. Thing is, the car's playing up and Sid's borrowed the van. Can you hang on another hour?'

'No! I've gotta get back for three.'

'What for?'

I kicked the big board. 'I just have to. Look, I'll try and hitch. I'll leave the sign.'

'It's only another hour.'

'Gotta run, Dad. Later.'

Green, Dark & Shady came out of my pockets, and into place. I crossed the road, where traffic was back in full flow, and held out a thumb. Ugly kids on back seats put out their tongues or stuck up two fingers. I gave them a variety of gestures back. Time ticked on, and I twitched by the road in desperation to keep my date. Finally a great beast of a Range Rover braked suddenly just ahead.

I ran along the verge and jumped in by the driver. 'Cheers,' I said. 'I'm heading for Wolf Hill.' I looked up, and met the blue eyes of Lady Standish, her dyed blonde hair long and loose. Her polo-shirt was wide open, so I got a shufty at the top of her breasts. She wore a white tennis skirt.

'Young Mr Ashburner!' she said.

'Oh. Hello. Thanks for stopping.'

'My husband's away, so we've been on a day trip. Hold tight.'

I belted up as we roared off. The twins were giggling on the back seat; a golden little boy and a golden girl. They were jabbing and tickling each other.

Lady Standish looked at them in the mirror. 'Elizabeth, Edward,' she said. 'Sit still, please.' She kept looking in that rear-view mirror as if to watch the kids, but it seemed like she was really checking on herself. She smoothed the make-up around her eyes. The car was filled with warm and musky perfumes. I wound my window down.

Lady Standish took out a vanity case, and drove along with her elbows on the wheel. She rubbed her lips, then dropped the case when a lorry hooted behind. As the car lurched, the twins screamed and laughed like this was a funfair.

'Sorry,' said Lady Standish. 'Could you hold this, please?' She passed me a small leather handbag. 'There's a picture inside that you might find interesting.'

On top of the vanity objects was a photo cut from a magazine. I took it out, and saw Lady Standish as she was maybe a decade ago, perhaps more. She wore a stylish pink dress that left her shoulders bare. It must have been from a fashion shoot, but the date had been clipped from the cutting.

'Wow,' I said.

Lady Standish slipped her feet out of bright tennis shoes, and pressed the pedals, each toenail blobbed with blue.

'That was in the *Sunday Times*,' she said. 'I'm doing another for them soon.'

'Brill. Anywhere exotic?'

'I hope so. England bores me so.'

I leaned on the open window. 'Yeah. It's so passé now.'

She didn't drop me at The Forge, but drove straight down to Harker Hall. 'Would you help me unload the car? I'll reward you.'

My heart gave a squeeze. 'You will?'

'Yes. A nice cool drink. I'm ready for one.'

'Ah.'

We sat in the car as the twins jumped out. Lady Standish looked at me, as if puzzled. 'For a muscular young man, you seem to hide yourself from the world.

What are those skin marks behind your glasses? Are they sunburns?' She leaned closer. I leaned away.

And then the twins began screaming on the doorstep. We both stared through the windscreen in shock. The little girl was pointing to a dead rooster.

TWENTY

I jumped out first with her ladyship close behind. The boy, Edward, had picked up a stick and was prodding the rooster's feathery body. The bird's eyes were still and startled. It already smelled fairly rank.

'Don't touch it!' Lady Standish ordered.

'It was here,' said Elizabeth, 'by the door.' Edward kicked it, so the rooster lay on one side as if asleep. Lady Standish turned to me. 'Do you recognize this bird? Is it the loud one from that farm behind us?'

'I think so. It looks old enough.'

'Was it left here to scare us?'

'Hard to say. Maybe it died of stress after you pressed charges.'

Lady Standish toed the bird. 'Please throw it away when you leave.' We went back to the car, and she gave me some heavy Marks & Spencer bags to carry. They were full of ready meals and boozy bottles.

It was cool in the kitchen of Harker Hall, where a big Aga cooker stood at the side. The walls were lined with copper cooking pans which looked unused. The twins went off upstairs with orders to wash their hands thoroughly. Lady Standish's fingers were shaking as she unpacked the shopping. She took out a fresh bottle of M & S vodka and poured herself a large glass over ice. She downed half of it, then handed me a cold Coke. 'Sorry,' she said. 'I'm in shock after seeing that dead beast.'

'Don't worry,' I said. 'It's how things get dealt with round here.'

Lady Standish took another long drink, gripped her blonde hair, and looked stressy. She laid that fashion photo of herself on the table.

I sipped my drink and looked at the picture. 'How old were you back then?' I asked. I knew right off it was the wrong thing to say. The difference between Lady Standish then and now was obvious, despite her make-up and manicures. She turned her back on me. It seemed there was to be no further reward from her. My clumsy question, and that minging rooster, had killed off any flirtation.

I took my leave and hurled the dead bird into the bushes on one side. Some fox would thank me later. As I glanced back indoors, Lady Standish held the vodka bottle over her glass and poured another generous shot.

'You're late,' said Angel, looking serious.

'Sorry. Had to unpack some bags for Lady Standish.'

'You're kidding! Did she mention my break-in at their place?'

'Nah. But that stuff you nicked could come in handy.'

We stood in the shadows of the dawn redwood tree. Angel wore the same grubby white dress as before, and her grungy boots. Her knees were scabby from climbing rough bark. She pointed up to her tree house and said, 'Wanna see what I've done?'

I rubbed my neck. 'Well, sure, but I thought I was meeting your folks.'

'Oh, yeah. OK, but with my parents you never know what to expect.'

I tumbled along eagerly, as Angel led the way through a dark maze of pines, where daylight seemed always in the distance. She took me further into the wood, along the ridge leading away from Wolf Hill. Towards the back of the forest the trees began to thin out, and there were patches of sunny bracken. Those green ferns were already browning in the dry summer. The soil below was baked to a crust.

Angel pointed to a low stone wall, topped with scraps of wire. 'Over there,' she said. On the other side lay lumpy meadows that were once dense woodlands, or farm land. Across the way I saw a clump of sycamores and guessed we were close to the farm squat. Sycamores were often planted around old houses as they gave good shelter. They had spreading branches, and big leaves to keep out strong winds.

Sure enough, there was a battered building among them. It stood by a stream that was hardly trickling. The land beyond was yellow with wild grasses.

The place was made of stone slabs and grey slates. What would have been a solid farmhouse in times past was now left open to rain and ruin. I'd been by it before, but never imagined anyone staying there.

'Sssh!' Angel hissed. 'They might be asleep.'

'Asleep? It's only four o'clock.'

She took my hand. It felt so small inside mine. 'They sometimes go to bed in the afternoon and make love,' she said softly. 'Let's creep inside.'

I stroked her fingers with my thumb. We went in through a door-shaped gap. The floors were covered in rubble, the walls crumbling. A stone staircase lay before us. Angel quietly took off her boots and I did the same, then we trod softly up the cold steps to a landing. Weeds and mosses were everywhere. There were two rooms in front of us, and an open space full of fallen slate on the right.

Angel tiptoed to a flaky wooden door, and put an ear to it. She stood there like a spy or a thief. I went up beside her. She whispered, 'Can you hear? Can you hear them?'

I pressed my head close to her face and the woodwork. I could only hear the nervous blood in my ears, and Angel's breathing.

'They're asleep,' she said. 'We can't disturb them now.'

'Where's your room?' I whispered. My heart was heavy with lust, and kicking like a wild horse. Angel pointed to the next door and opened it a crack. I peeked inside and caught a glimpse of girl's clothes and a mattress.

'Not now,' Angel said. She pulled me away, and my desires were forced to fade. We went back downstairs to get our boots, and crossed the stream, before Angel pulled me down into a patch of tall wild flowers.

She kneeled next to me. Her oval face, with only a hint of pink, was up close. I blew a breath at her slim nose and plump lips. She seemed so elfin beside the big bear I had grown into. And as she edged her body against mine, I wanted to sigh and explode. I nuzzled into her waterfall hair. She brushed aside my own heavy locks.

Angel whispered, 'Be brave. I can't love you if I don't know what's under there.'

TWENTY-ONE

She removed my baseball cap, and placed it on the grass beside her. Then she slowly slipped off my dark hood. It fell backwards onto my shoulders. I felt like a leafless tree without my coverings and tried to grope the hood back into place.

Angel held my hands down firmly. Then with soft fingers she began to ease off my heavy glasses. I pulled away. 'Hey,' she breathed. 'No going back. Not this time.'

'OK. Just don't be scared at what you see.'

I let Angel take away the dark specs, through which I had viewed the world in artificial light for so long. The pupils of my eyes went tight. I blinked at the circles before me. And finally Angel smoothed away my mass of twisted hair. I closed my eyes as she examined my red stripes for the first time. Her touch was ticklish and soothing. She stroked a scar, as if to wipe it away like a tear. One finger traced the bare notch in an eyebrow. I bowed my head when Angel sat back in silence.

After an age I heard her sigh like the breeze. 'You poor thing,' she said. 'Years of lost living, just for this.'

I raised my sun-dazzled eyes. 'You mean, it's not so gross?'

Angel flipped aside the hair over her right eye. With hands clasped, she stared me out until I looked away. She said, 'It's not gross at all. You're really quite peachy.'

Like an addict I reached for Green, Dark & Shady. Angel grabbed them off me. 'Leave them,' she said. 'You're going home without all this. I bet nobody gives you a second look.'

I was used to roaming Appletree Wood with my face bared, as it was the only place I could shake off everything and be free. But slogging back to The Forge with the chance of people rambling around was another thing.

We headed back to Cherry's hut where Angel hunted around in my wigwam of clay and ferns, then came out with a bag of charcoal. She sat on a beer crate, tugged up her white dress and fanned her bare legs. I sat cross-legged and stared at the flickers of bliss on show.

Angel had this hot and musky scent about her that made me wild. She held up a piece of my charcoal. Like an artist applying make-up, she slowly streaked her face. The coal was fresh, and pitch-dark from burning. She put several stripes down her cheeks, then across her forehead. The black was such a contrast to her bloodless skin. When she finished with two lines of scratchy charcoal down her neck, she looked like a pagan made ready for battle.

'Done,' she said. 'So now we're both marked. And now . . . you belong to me.'

I reached out for her, grasping at white cotton and warm legs.

'Let's find a stream,' said Angel. She jumped up. 'I'm thirsty.'

I rubbed my eyes and led her downhill, hacking brambles with my billhook. I was lost in a haze of summer sounds and blinding love. As I stroked Angel's fingertips, she brushed hers back against mine. This made me grow bolder and put an arm around her slight waist. It was like holding some forest pixie who might dissolve into sudden bubbles.

At the stream you could see through the last line of trees. I pointed to the gleaming barley field below. 'That's where it all started,' I said. 'Five summers ago.'

We sat on a patch of green and silky moss. 'What happened to the other kids?' Angel asked. 'The ones who were there that day?'

'Some went to different schools,' I said. 'The Wilson boys hardly seemed to go at all – too busy keeping their farm going. I sometimes see Molly Hatton, the one who pulled those big sacks over me. She's always riding something, a horse or a moped.'

I cupped my hands in the stream, and lifted out clear water. I offered it to Angel, and she lapped from my fingers like a kitten. She licked the last drops away, making my blood pump up.

'Let me try,' she said. She knelt forward, the toes of her boots on dry earth. Seconds later, she gave me the cup of her palms. I drank the cold water like it was precious. My tongue stroked salty skin, and Angel giggled.

She lay back with closed eyes. 'We stayed on an Irish island once,' she said. 'And you know what the boys there said when they felt randy? They said their spuds were boiling! I never forgot that.'

'Oh, OK,' I said. 'How about, my charcoals are glowing? I think that's the same.'

Angel looked at me, not blinking. 'Are they glowing?'

'They sure are.'

Angel stood up and brushed away a few black ants. 'I have to go. I'm away with my parents to a travellers' fair. Sorry they were crashed out before, but that's how they are. And don't go to the squat without me, yeah? No one's meant to know about it.'

'Right. So that's it then, yeah? You're running off again. When you back?'

'Soon. And then we'll go riding with my parents, on the new horses we're getting.'

Angel stepped over to me, then got down on her knees. 'Close your eyes,' she whispered. And as I did so, I felt hot hands on my forehead. Then they slipped into my wild locks. Soon came the brush of Angel's lips, and the sudden taste of her tongue. I reached out blindly for her long hair, trying to drag her down beside me. I gasped and sighed, but then she flew away softly, like a nightbird.

I looked at myself in the bathroom mirror at home. Could I really be 'peachy' like Angel said? After the farm accident, my face scabbed over then scarred. The skin knitted slowly back as dark pink lines, but the 'Red Stripe' nickname stuck.

I couldn't shake off the fixed image I had, from the first time I saw those marks. Then, at the age of thirteen, I had a growth spurt, which shot me up taller than other kids my age. By fifteen I was a six-footer with a barrel chest. But even then I sat at the back of classes, head in hands, and staring down.

For the first time in days, I took a bath to wash away the grot. My soaked hair felt heavy under its weight of water. Lying back, I began to worry about this whole thing going on with Angel. It wasn't just doubts that she could ever find me attractive. It was more a fear that she'd taken pity on me, or was only leading me on.

I heaved myself out of the bath, and got ready to shave. Even then, I paused before the steamed-up bathroom mirror, as if rubbing it clean might bring all my doubts to light again. With a finger, I wrote Angel's name in a heart shape on the cloudy glass.

I wiped it away with a sponge, and hunted for one of Dad's razors.

TWENTY-TWO

Every day I checked our mail, which arrived about noon, hoping for good news from the heritage fund. I had heard about grants that were given to people who kept traditional crafts alive. Before my school days were over I'd started to apply for funding, with a mission to burn charcoal in the old style. I made a case for turning Appletree into a pure habitat, where nothing grotty would be shoved into the soil. Plant and animal life would thrive, I promised.

'Samson,' my mother snapped. 'There's no letters for you, but there's a blockage in the ladies loo. You'll have to use the toilet brush.'

'I'd rather use your head,' I muttered.

'What?'

'Nothing. What time does the *Evening Post* arrive?'

Mum waddled over to the kitchen table. 'It's just come. What do you want it for?'

I grabbed the paper and went to the Letters page, scanning every printed protest about dog fouling in Barrow and Salvation Army appeals. But my hoax written as the Cumbrian Phoenix was nowhere. I threw the paper aside.

Mum said, 'A load of rubbish on the cover. Some silly army of vandals.'

I flipped the *Evening Post* over and my heart quickened. A hot flush raced across my face and neck. This was the front-page headline, in big screaming print:

CUMBRIAN 'ARMY' THREATENS SECOND HOMES

I read the story with growing stress.

Members of a 'People's Army' have threatened to attack new holiday homes in the Lakes. A letter received by the Evening Post *says the army boasts over a hundred members.*

They claim that newcomers have pushed property prices so high that locals can't afford to live where they grew up.

Cumbria Police are investigating. A spokesperson said: 'We take all threats of this nature seriously. We ask holiday home owners to be extra vigilant, and if they see anything suspicious to report it.'

Forensic experts are now studying the typed letter, signed on behalf of the 'Army' by the 'Cumbrian Phoenix'. Police believe that the 'Phoenix' may be a Grade A anarchist, or eco-terrorist. They have asked for any information regarding this individual to be passed on to them.

Mum's voice broke through the crashing in my skull. 'It'll be some nasty jailbird, out on bail for beating up old ladies. Pass those eggs. Samson? Are you deaf?'

I fumbled for the eggs. 'Wake up, dreamer,' said Mum. 'At least you look a bit happier today. You've even washed your hair.'

I stood at the sink, scrubbing jacket potatoes, and after the first shock had worn off I began to feel chuffed, if a bit scared. But what's more, I could make sure Lord Hugo Standish saw it and give him worries over his scheme.

Even better, I could tell Angel Obscura about this. After our blissful kiss yesterday I had floated on clouds. My role as the Cumbrian Phoenix might be the final seal of her love for me. I could hardly stay still for joy and couldn't wait for her to return.

It was closing time at The Forge, and we'd had a dreary night. The evening had been so hot that people cancelled their bookings to stay at home and have barbecues. I could make a tidy penny from my charcoal industry, if left alone.

I stuffed the *Evening Post* front page up my shirt, and hung around by the pub. Dad's slogan for today was chalked on a signboard outside.

WELCOME TO THE FORGE
THAI MIDGET BOXING TONIGHT!

I heard a flush in the men's bogs, which backed onto the side wall. And then one of our regulars came climbing out of the toilet window. It was Tipsy Sid, known for his way of walking like a drunk, even when sober. After every few steps he gave a little hop, skip and a jump. He saw me and said, 'Your old man's got his home brew out. I can't face another drop. Can't you tell him to stop?'

'No point,' I said. 'He'll not stop until he's cracked it.'

Sid shook his head, and went down the lane with his giddy walk. Within the next two minutes, another three old-timers had scrambled through the toilet window rather than face Dad's latest brewing disaster.

Dad came out with a glass, scratching his curly hair. 'Where's everyone gone?'

'No idea. What you got there?'

Dad explained it was an ancient recipe he'd made, where you pass beer over the dregs of mashed damsons. 'Have a try.'

I took a cautious sniff and swig. An aroma of recycled bottle banks, and a taste of cough medicine.

'Not far off,' I said. 'What time's the midget boxing start?'

It was half past eleven before I snuck down the drive of Harker Hall. The square grey house looked dismal in the dusk. I scampered under the cover of bushes towards three huge cars. Kneeling behind one, I saw Lady Standish come downstairs.

She stood before a dark window, her hair piled high. Then one hand went flat under her chin, the other pressed her scalp. She thrust out her face and studied herself in the window for ages. At last she pushed upward on the frame and leaned out, taking deep breaths. I peeped over the car's bonnet as she gripped her hair and whispered loudly, 'Get me away from here. Don't leave me like this.'

My skin iced over until I realized she was only talking to herself. Even then, my flesh stayed cold for minutes after, as Lady Standish stood there muttering. At last she sat down at the table, in the darkness, her white face towards me. This scuppered my plans for sneaking the press article through the front letterbox. From there Lady Standish might hear it, or see me leave.

I crawled through the walled archway and headed round the back. A long expanse of lawn lay ahead, down to some distant woods. There were signs of work on a circular helipad.

I wanted to find a living room to shove the *Evening Post* front page into, and maybe have a nose around. The third window along had a soft light. On hands and knees I went down the grass. The newspaper rustled under my shirt like a paper vest.

My body was below the third white sill, its window open at the bottom. Very slowly I eased myself up and had a look inside. But what I saw there made me freeze with shock.

Angel Obscura was rooting through some documents on a desk. She wore a black shirt and combat trousers, like a soldier on patrol. At every creak inside the house she glanced anxiously at the door behind her. The room was large, with leather sofas, like a study or a posh office. Angel nicked some keys from a jacket left lying on the couch. She opened a locked drawer and sifted through piles of papers.

Voices from beyond grew suddenly louder. I was about to rap on the window, and lift it to let Angel escape. But she shoved the papers back, locked the drawer and put away the keys. And just before the door burst open, she dived across into a big armchair.

TWENTY-THREE

Angel was caught red-handed, yet she sat upright in a plush chair, looking so calm. It was midnight, and too dark for me to be seen from the lit room. Even so my head stayed at just a level to watch events unfold. The window was open enough for me to hear a clock ticking indoors.

Lord Standish came into the room, but didn't shout in outrage at Angel's presence. He simply eased himself into another chair, his left cheek in profile to me. He and Angel sat in silence, glaring at each other. Angel's face was hard and frosty. Standish's jaw was twitching, like someone trying to stay in control. The two stared each other out until Standish finally spoke. 'What are you doing in here? This is my private office.'

Angel gave a bony shrug. 'So?'

'So, you don't come in here without permission.'

Angel sounded bored. 'You go into my place without asking.'

'With good reason,' said Standish. 'Until you can be trusted, we will continue to search for evidence of your behaviour. Or until you start pulling yourself together.'

Angel looked up at the grand ceiling, with its white carvings. 'Blah blah,' she said. 'Can I go now? I'm tired.'

Standish stood up. 'Tired from what? Not from hard work. You promised to catch up on your studies this summer, but your mother says you often disappear for half the day.' He walked over to the window and pushed it open further. I bobbed down by the grey wall. The room's door banged again, and when I dared look back I saw Lady Standish there too.

'Hello, Mumsy,' said Angel. 'Let's play Happy Families.'

Lady Standish sat on the sofa in a pink nightdress. She spoke to Angel with sorrow. 'Don't get angry at me, darling.'

Angel stood up and tried to leave, but Standish blocked the way.

'Not yet,' he said. 'Not until a few rules have been drawn up.'

Angel made a big show of outrage, tossing her white mane like a horse. She sat down again, huddled up, and closed her eyes.

'Firstly,' said Standish, 'as agreed, you will spend a few days with Sister Clayton. You will be driven to the Catholic summer school tomorrow, where you can catch up on some course work.

'Secondly, in September you will start afresh at St Mary's. We'll see if they can manage your various problems. The staff there are trained to work with young people like you. There's even a chance you might pass some exams.'

Angel stared blindly towards me. 'What else?'

'Thirdly,' said Standish, pacing like a great thinker, 'you will spend any spare time this summer helping your mother. There'll be no more gadding off to wherever. Is all of that quite clear?'

Angel nodded dumbly. Standish looked powerful in a stripy shirt, dark trousers and gold watch. A ticking clock inside filled the sudden silence.

'Fine,' said Standish. 'Much as you might hate me now, I do this for your own good. If you can manage the next two years, and start improving, then maybe we'll talk about university. Maybe.' He left the room.

His wife lay with eyes closed, then sat up at a noise from above. 'The twins,' she said, stumbling to her feet. 'They're awake. Wait here, Victoria.' She left the room too, trailing pink silk. Angel stayed tucked up on the chair, and began to scratch herself wildly all over. Finally she lay on the carpet out of sight, but I heard weeping. She coughed and choked like someone retching.

I dropped back against the wall, below the sill. I rubbed my fingers down my face. And then my heart broke open like a snapped branch.

I tore back through the archway, down the drive, and out into the lane. Turning left, I ran up to the old ivy cottage, where I rested my head and hands against cool leaves. My body heaved as I gulped for breath. I went around the cottage and up the old bridleway to Appletree Wood, as I had a thousand times before, but never with such chaos inside. Only when I was at Cherry's hut, laid out on his old bed, did I give in to the tears. My anger boiled up and howled into the darkness.

'You bitch!' I screamed. 'You lied!'

I rubbed my flooding cheeks. 'Why?' I sobbed. 'I'd have done anything for you.' Fragments of memory, like clues to a crime, came to haunt me. Angel's rich and exotic perfume; the posh way she washed her feet in my drinking bucket before going home; the warning not to visit the squat without her; the vanishing and appearing at odd moments; her imagined parents.

I thought of Angel painting herself with my charcoal earlier. What had she said afterwards? *So now we're both marked. And now . . . you belong to me.* It already felt like a scene from a more innocent time.

The forest was a soothing grotto all around me. Every creature seemed to hold its breath. Silence and darkness were as thick as thieves.

It was half an hour before my spirit calmed itself. My tears were dry and cold. I sat up slowly, like a tired old man, with that *Evening Post* front page still under my shirt. I stashed it in the tin box I kept inside Cherry's hut, then shoved it back under its heap of bracken. It held some other things my mother wouldn't like to find, and also my old title deed. The box was too heavy and awkward to drag elsewhere, even if I found a suitable place, but I knew it was time to shift the thing. The document inside it was so valuable to me.

I couldn't think of resting yet, and wandered around Appletree Wood, weaving through the solid bodies of oak, ash and sycamore. I came to a small clearing where the moonlight found a gap. Before me was a huge upended tree, like a dark spook. Its spidery roots were wrapped in sods of dry soil.

About one in the morning I crept back to my hut, still unable to sleep but calmer now. I lit two candle lamps and put them by me. From a bag I chose a large piece of charcoal that I hadn't yet chopped up. It was the length of my forearm. I began working on it with a small penknife used for stripping thin hazel branches.

Where could I hide that bloody tin box? Where?

The chunk of charcoal slowly took shape. It was easy enough to see by the candle lights. My blade scraped and sculpted, until at last I was done.

Holding it to the yellow light, I saw the rough shape of an angel. Its wings were carved like the two halves of a broken heart. As the flames burned low in my old lamps, it looked like a saintly voodoo doll. I held it before me, and spoke softly.

'Hey, Angel. Why all the lies and trickery?'

I shook the charcoal figurine. Its little dark head stared back.

'Hey, Angel. What's up, rich bitch? You just get bored this summer, and need a lonely plaything?'

I stabbed two eye holes into the head with my knife's point.

'That's better. You can see me for real now.'

Opening one of the lamps, I charred the angel's head on a flame until it smoked.

'So now we're both marked. And now . . . you belong to me. You'll see.'

TWENTY-FOUR

Early next morning, with my heart in turmoil, I headed back down to The Forge. I let myself in quietly, and made it to my bedroom unseen. My soft pillow became Angel's impish body, which I hugged and caressed before sitting up and punching fierce dents into it. Then I began to steel myself for the battles ahead. Before going downstairs, I put my cap and sunglasses in the pockets of my zip-up hoodie. Now I couldn't even trust Angel's sugary words about how I looked, so I was back to square one.

We had some daily papers delivered to The Forge, for punters to read over their pints. They were on the kitchen table when I went down for late breakfast. I wore my LEGALIZE DA 'ERB T-shirt, which I rated as Mum's second least favourite of mine.

'And a good day to you,' she whined. She'd dyed her hair with what could have been red ink. It lay flat like a man's hairpiece. She waddled across and grabbed my locks. 'Time for a chop,' she said. 'Where's your billhook?'

'Get knotted,' I said, pushing her away.

'Ooooh! What happened to Mr Smiley? Was yesterday your one nice day of the year?'

'Yep. That's it. Normal nastiness from now on.'

'Hmmph. You'll be off with those nutters in the Phoenix Army next, or whatever. It's all over the nationals now.'

My stomach lurched like I was seasick. I grabbed the *Sun*, open on the table. It was the main story on page seven, nicked from the *Evening Post*'s version. This was the loud headline:

LOONIES IN THE LAKES!

A maniac terror group in Cumbria has issued death threats against second-home owners. The People's Army says they will burn all new holiday houses. Led by the so-called 'Cumbrian Phoenix', the group . . .

There was something similar among the *Star*'s gossip and scandals. Page nine . . .

IT'S THE FARMY ARMY!

War has been declared on the Lake District's posh frocks by a fanatic known as the 'Cumbrian Phoenix'. Along with over a hundred others, the Phoenix is ready to burn rich oiks out of house and home.

Police in Cumbria are already hunting the Phoenix after he issued his threats via a local paper. They believe he may be a serial offender, with a grudge against the well-to-do. His 'People's Army' wants an end to new holiday homes, built for loaded incomers who drive out the locals.

And so it went on. It said the cops were examining the letter, and its 'badly faked writing on the envelope'. My fingerprints would be all over it, but they'd have to check half the county's first to reach mine.

My head throbbed with raw nerves. It felt like the hot sun outside was a spotlight searching for me. Any second now it would burn through the ceiling, and sirens would scream at the door. Five years in prison would follow, with hairy primates trying to rape me in the showers.

'When you've finished ogling Page Three girls,' said Mum, 'there's a load of peas need shelling.'

'Use tinned ones,' I said, and got whacked with raw rhubarb.

I put on Green, Dark & Shady that evening, before going up to Appletree Wood, where the earth mover still sat like a museum piece. Its tyres had been replaced at last. Soon after, I was in the meadows leading to that old farmhouse, where I once thought Angel and her parents were squatting.

The stony ruin loomed behind spreading sycamores. Inside, I looked around at the rotting timbers and grey rock. Going up the staircase it felt like a haunted home, where bats might swoop out of every crack.

I opened the creaky door to where Angel said her parents had been asleep. The room was empty except for an old ladder and some rope. I kicked open the door to

Angel's room and at last found signs of the life she'd let me imagine. There was a white blanket, a sleeping bag and a cushion. Candles and matches lay burned and used. I picked up an empty bottle of Bacardi, and some cigarette papers.

I sat on the bed looking at all this debris. Feeling a lump underneath, I pulled out a bundle of grubby clothes, and the white dress with flower patterns. How many times had she slipped from one set of garments into another, to fool me or her family?

Then my hand fell on a book, a diary she kept under the mattress. It was black and hand-sized. The front pages seemed to be written about Angel's real life, and the back ones about her imagined existence. I read some scraps at the beginning, dated months earlier.

Hugo on the rampage. Came blazing into school like the freak he is. Went to my study and packed my bags. Marched me through the school yard to the car. Everyone watching. Every girl stopped and stared ...

Mother on the bottle again, but only when Hugo away. Twins driving me nuts. Don't the little sods ever sleep? Drank the dregs of Mother's sweet sherry ...

Stuck in darkest Hampshire with a sad home-tutor. Am sure he stole a pair of my knickers. Found him grubbing about in my room. Said he was checking my bookshelf. Top shelf more likely with him. And hasn't he got any toothpaste? Mr Death Breath!

The end pages were undated. I read some fragments, written in fancy italics.

Tonight I am lying on a hillside far from any town. I can see the Plough constellation among the stars. Seven twinkles of light, and a line through two of them pointing nearly to the Pole Star ...

I am so glad to live a life of open travel. There is nowhere beyond reach, or beyond my dreams ...

The night is cold, but I am wrapped in blankets by a camp fire. The mountains beyond are grey with old snow ...

I will never grow tired of life, not like the other people, with such freedoms all around me ...

In the morning the sun will rise and blind my eyes. We will move on ...

There was no mention of me anywhere. I slid the book back under the mattress, and left the crumbling farmhouse. Night was closing in over Appletree Wood and the route back to the pitstead was shadowy. My mind was trying to make sense of things, so I got out that doll-sized charcoal angel I'd left in Cherry's hut. With my billhook, I carefully slit the figurine in half, from top to bottom. Sitting by the glow of candle lamps, I held one part in each hand. I spoke to the left one first.

'So, now. Are you the side of Angel that likes me? And is that the same Angel who wants to save my woodland?'

I turned to the dark lump in my right hand. 'Does

that make you the half that wants to get even with your daddy? The same half that's been tricking me?'

I pressed the two parts together. 'Talk to each other! Why can't you be one person?' The broken angel stared blackly back at me, its wings drooping.

'You know what I think? Yeah, I don't know what to think. But I need your help, Angel. You owe me.'

TWENTY-FIVE

The next morning I woke in my sleeping bag to a terrible sound. A heavy engine vroomed in the distance, as that earth mover suddenly rattled the branches. It took half a minute for me to get up and make a path to the machine. I lobbed a rock that pinged off its engine.

The driver stopped and got out. It was Gregson, his pink head glowing. 'Aha,' he said. 'It's the monkey man himself.'

I wanted to seem fearless but the piggy eyes staring back were brutal. There was no brain behind them to reason with.

I said, 'What the hell you up to?'

Gregson came closer, all yellow jacket and big boots. 'I'm doing my job.' He stuck up a finger. 'And anyone trying to stop me can suck this.'

'You're on my land,' I said. 'I told you before.'

Gregson kicked some ferns that seemed to bow before him. He wasn't tall but had a muscular power. 'This land belongs to Harker Hall,' he said. 'It goes with the property and that property is now Lord Standish's. So, you gonna leave quietly, or go the hard way?'

I gave a false laugh. 'You're the business, mate.

The absolute biz. I own Appletree Wood, from that charcoal burner's hut back there. It was agreed and signed by my great-grandpa and the old Harker geezer.'

Gregson smacked a fly, and spat. 'Where's your proof?'

'Wait there,' I said. 'Try not to destroy anything.'

I legged it back to Cherry's hut where the original document lay in my tin box. A few minutes later I thrust it in Gregson's face. He chewed gum and read it with a smile.

'This'll really hold up in court,' he laughed. 'It all means total jack. Here, take it back to your wigwam. You got any Injuns in there?'

'Yeah. But they ain't gonna scalp you, mate. You'd need some hair first.'

Gregson gave an evil wink. 'OK, Scar Face. Just clear your stuff by tomorrow, or I'll crush the lot.'

With a furious finger I pointed at his previous trail of damage. 'Those were hazel trees, dumbster. Hazels grown to make charcoal, grown by me and looked after by me. It takes years for them to produce that many shoots.'

'Don't matter,' said Gregson. 'Half this timber's coming down.'

'For what, huh?'

Gregson got mouthy and loud. 'That ain't your business, dummy sucker. Whatever Lord Standish does here is private. He can build a motorway if he wants to.'

I backed away as Gregson barged forward. 'Over my dead body,' I said.

'Fine. I'll bury you facing your dead-end pub.' He farted and left. I stood there, ready to throw myself in front of the digger if it moved an inch. But instead of hauling himself up to the driver's cabin, Gregson walked straight past his machine and back out to the bridleway. I followed him to the woodland's edge, and watched as he pulled out a phone and pressed its dial pad.

I cracked my fists together in triumph. This was a victory of sorts, if just for now.

I fled back to the pitstead and lit a pile of stalks, fanning the flames so their fumes went high up through the clearing. This was a smoke signal of war. The Cumbrian Phoenix was ready to rise.

Nobody bothered me the rest of that day. With my mobile turned off, and The Forge so quiet, nothing much was required of me. I was hot and bored, but still held my ground.

Next morning I got up in Appletree with a plan to block the entrance to my wood. Back at The Forge, I padded quietly along the upstairs passage to get washed. It's then I heard someone weeping in my parents' room. It was my mother; I could tell by the wheezing between her sobs, and that grinding of teeth.

Then came Dad's voice. He sounded upset too. 'Don't

cry, my love,' he said gently. 'We're not finished yet. Not quite.'

I paused outside their door, which was open a touch. My parents sat on the bed, their backs to me, arms around each other. They looked like a cartoon couple, with my mother's wiggy red hair and Dad in his old vest. They rocked each other like little kids. A pile of letters and papers lay on the duvet. Dad kissed Mum's hamster cheek, then she held his curly head on her shoulder. His face slid to her flabby breasts. She stroked his hair, picking out bits of dandruff, like an old orang-utan.

Inside our workshed I found enough wood and nails to knock up a signpost. This is what I painted on it in bold red:

PRIVATE PROPERTY
KEEP OUT!

I lugged it up to Appletree Wood, as the sun grilled me for breakfast. But when I got to the end of the bridleway, where my wood opened out, another sign had gone up. It was done with professional print, in black letters. It said:

PRIVATE PROPERTY!
KEEP OUT!

Pulling out this warning sign I shoved my own in its

place, hauled the other away, and dumped it onto last night's pitstead ashes. I made a morning bonfire and toasted bread over its flames.

All I did was sit by the fire, or brood inside Cherry's hut when the heat grew intense.

And that's where Lord Standing Joke found me when he pushed through the forest that morning. Gregson must have told him about my claim. I stood with my hackles raised, and my dark hood in place. I was like some crazy hermit, ready to fight for his home among the mountain caves.

TWENTY-SIX

'Show me this document,' said Standish. He looked quite human in a T-shirt and jeans. His rocky jaw was unshaven with light stubble.

'Close your eyes then,' I said.

'What?'

'Close your eyes and turn round. It's hidden.'

With the smile of a tolerant parent, Standish did as I asked. From that heavy tin box, I fished out the worn paper with its faded writing. 'Here,' I said. 'Contest it if you like but how's it gonna look? Your big business against a poor boy's heritage.'

Standish gave the paper a serious study. 'I'm not quite the tyrant you imagine,' he said. 'I accept this deed was made in good faith, although the youngest child rarely has any legal claims. But this wood belongs to Harker Hall. My architect's plan names this place as Ashburner's Wood, and includes it as part of the hall's land.' He handed the document back.

'Hah. Ashburner's my family name,' I said. 'Sounds like some old architect renamed the wood for us, after my deed was written. But we've always used its old name, Appletree. And what's more, my charcoal business is based here.'

Standish looked concerned. 'What? You mean you're running a real business on this site?'

'Oh, yeah. Quite a good one. '

'Right. So, you have accounts and invoices that the courts could see?'

'Don't need figures,' I said. 'It's quite fluid really, the business. Sort of organic.'

Standish rubbed his eyes. He looked at Cherry's hut, and then at his burning signpost. 'OK,' he said. 'Here's a deal of sorts. You find another site for your charcoal, somewhere a good distance away. And as a gesture of goodwill, I will pay a lump sum into your family's business account. What you all do with it is your concern.'

I thought of Angel testing me one time, and how I'd boasted I would turn down five million quid for Appletree Wood. Well, here was her real dad offering real money.

'Um, what sort of lump sum?'

'I hadn't decided on a ballpark figure,' said Standish. 'But let's go for ... say ... twenty thousand Twenty grand from one neighbour to another. Deal or no deal?'

I'd be lying if I said that human greed didn't flash inside me. I'd never lacked for food and shelter, only for motherly love and close friendship. But I wanted things beyond money: I wanted a girlfriend and I wanted real life. I wanted my scars to vanish completely and my adult life to begin. And I knew that most of

Standish's cash would get swallowed up by The Forge's debts.

'No deal,' I said coldly. 'Tell me why you want this forest so badly.'

'Well, I'm trying to have a summer house built here,' said Standish. 'Perfect spot. So think long and hard before you turn me down. Think of your parents too.'

He turned away, back across the clearing, leaving this hint of a threat. Would he go and see my folks right then? I thought maybe not. Far better to tempt a teenage boy, and let the dream of money fester in his brain for a while.

Back at the pub, Dad was hauling out the signboard with his latest chalked slogan:

WELCOME TO THE FORGE

NO TEAM COLOURS!

NO CHANTING CHIMPS!

'We'll need you here today,' said Dad. 'There's a coach load of Japanese tourists booked in for lunch. Go and give your mother a hand.'

The menu had been adapted to suit the guests. They were gonna get a chance to 'Eat the View' with a taste of their home thrown in. These were Mum's daily specials, over which she had been slaving all morning:

Roast shoulder of Wolf Hill lamb,
with soy-ginger sauce;

Crispy Cumbrian pork,
with sweet and sour rhubarb;

Barbecued Duddon shellfish,
with chilli-lime dressing.

Our barbecue was even set up outside near the kitchen door. Mum was shaking the last charcoals onto it from one of my carriers. 'Damn,' she said. 'There's not enough.'

'Hang on,' I said, and legged it back to Appletree to fetch my last load. Back at The Forge I dumped them on the home-made brick barbie, adding bunches of our garden herbs for aroma and flavour.

'Ta,' said Mum. 'How much?'

'Still free,' I said. 'Just bear in mind how much I save you with my supplies, and how much I could make from my own charcoal business.'

That shut her up for all of ten seconds. 'Samson! Simmer a pot of rhubarb, not too much water and sugar, then whiz half in the blender and stir that into the remainder. The coach is getting here at one. And check on that pork in the oven.'

I opened the stove and black fumes blew out. 'Uughh! When was this last cleaned?'

'Yesterday. The damned thing keeps playing up and

we can't afford a new one. Not unless you've found a rich fairy godmother in your wood.'

When the coach party arrived, their Japanese guide got off and was greeted by Dad. The visitors all piled out, wearing red Manchester United football tops, on their way down to Old Trafford for a stadium tour. One of them noticed Dad's chalked sign by the wall. He asked the guide, in Japanese, what it said. The guide stared at it too, then jabbed a finger at Dad. He spoke angrily in his own language, before turning to the group of thirty footie fans and ranting on.

Dad smacked his forehead, gazing in horror at his jokey slogan:

NO TEAM COLOURS!
NO CHANTING CHIMPS!

The mood quickly got nasty as the guide turned on Dad. 'You don't want us here? No? We wear our team colours down to Manchester today. And you say we are all dirty chimps, chanting rude songs! Yes?'

Some of the crowd were already getting back on the coach. Dad ran around trying to calm them as they each got a translation of his sign. 'It was only a laugh! Honest, they never said you were a football party. Let me explain.'

But the tour guide had seen enough, and ushered his

red-shirted mob back on board. 'We go elsewhere,' he said. 'Never return.'

The coach pulled into the narrow lane and Dad ran after it banging the sides and windows. 'Come back! Please! Lunch on the house!'

His only reply was a face full of exhaust fumes. He sank to his knees by the hedgerow as I patted his back.

He turned to me, and whispered, 'Who's gonna tell your mother? Will you?'

'Nah. You're her husband and the bar manager.'

Dad was still whispering. 'She'll hit the flaming roof.'

I squeezed my old man's shoulders. 'Be brave. Have a nice pint first.'

The rumpus that kicked off a minute later in our kitchen could probably be heard down on Wilson's farm.

TWENTY-SEVEN

Dad spent much of that day hiding out in his brewing shed. Mum raged and wheezed at both of us. I went into Dad's shed too, where his home-brew was bubbling in copper vats and plastic pipes. He siphoned off a glass of his latest effort. 'Sort of a Pilsner,' he said.

The aroma struck me as a bit dodgy. It was like when your washing machine burps through the kitchen sink. And the taste was too metallic, like sucking the pins of a plug. But after the first kick came a hint of promise, as the flavour mellowed out into something quite decent. 'Hmm,' I said. 'Your best yet.'

'Yeah? Not quite there, but worth trying even if we are on borrowed time.'

'Sure,' I said. 'It's hard – we're just so remote here.'

'Aye, I know. My only regulars are a bunch of half-pint grumps. Could do with more homes in Wolf Hill, maybe a few more rich ones.'

I drained the glass. 'Yeah, but hang on, Dad. You don't want a load of holiday homers churning up the place.'

'Don't I? Don't I just.'

'But what if it means tearing up the woodland? Doesn't that matter?'

One of the cauldrons began smoking like a witchy brew. Dad turned a control and wrote something on his wallchart. 'I'm not sure it matters what people like us think,' he said. 'Survival is our biggest aim.'

'Well, it ain't enough,' I said. 'There's a war on between the haves and have-nots.'

'Steady, son. You're sounding like that Phoenix nutter. You seen today's *Evening Post*? Here.'

I looked at the inside page headline:

POLICE HOME IN ON 'CUMBRIAN PHOENIX'

Local police have made a breakthrough in their search for a green terrorist who made arson threats against new holiday homes. They have traced the source of the letter to south Cumbria, and the area between Coniston and Broughton. Further inquiries are being made . . .

That's all I could read without shivering. The hunt was on. I could almost hear the baying hounds as I fled through Appletree Wood. I could hear my mother in court, wheezing and grinding, as the judge sent me down. I'd share a cell with some child molester from Glasgow, who would wait eagerly for lights out.

'Samson? You finished with that paper? Tipsy Sid likes looking at the Night Clubbing pages. Can't think why.'

'It's them photos of girls on theme nights,' I said. 'The ones dressed up as tarts and vicars.'

*

We put the Japanese specials on the menu that evening, but hardly anyone turned up to eat them. 'Why waste all this food?' I said. 'Just do a barbecue every night. I've got plenty of coals for burning.'

'Wonderful, Samson,' said Mum. 'When we're ready to go down the fast-food line I'll let you know.'

'It's not just for fast food. You can do steaming, smoking, baking.'

She knew I was right and that it made sense, but the stubborn ewe wasn't for changing. Not even when the vultures were hovering for our blood.

I went up to Appletree Wood and Cherry's hut that night. At some point the earth mover had vanished. Several beech trees near the bridleway still bore daubs of white spray paint, probably to mark them out for felling.

It was after ten o'clock when I headed home. As I loped uphill, Standish was walking ahead of me. He could only be heading to The Forge to ask my parents why their stupid son was turning down his money.

As he went through the front door, I crept in behind. Standish went along the stone corridor, and then stooped to his right into our tiny front bar.

'A pint of Tirril bitter, landlord,' he said. 'And one for yourself.'

Splash . . . squirt . . . creak. 'There you go, sir,' said Dad. 'That's four eighty.'

'Thank you. Good health.'

'The same to you, sir. And might I ask, do I have the honour of addressing Lord Standish? We had news of your arrival, sir, in our small community.'

Dad was really slapping it on. Lick, lick, slime, slurp. I stuck two fingers down my throat, then edged outside. And with Standing Joke having his royal butt kissed, now might be the only chance I got. I snuck away to Harker Hall, down its dusky drive, through the walled archway by the house and along the side. There might be a way to sneak into Standish's study and have a rifle through his papers. The ones Angel had stolen from her father were vital, but there must be more that I could use. Even if Standish made a legal claim on Appletree Wood, its trees lay just inside the Lake District National Park. He still might need permission to fell them.

I knelt below the study, its window open at the bottom. I stood up slowly then sank down in shock. Lady Standish was curled up on the sofa ahead of me. Her face looked a ghastly grey colour, as if she was a corpse. Then I realized she must be wearing some sort of mud pack, caked on heavily. Only her eyes were visible, staring out like blue jewels from sludge. She wore just a long shirt and white knickers.

She was on the phone and I realized she was talking to Angel. Standish must have carried out his promise to pack her off to that study school.

'Darling, I know . . . I know. Victoria, your father's

powers go beyond either of us. If he wants you sent away . . . Yes, I realize that . . . No, they don't call them mental homes any more. I will speak to your father . . . But you haven't been well, darling. Not for a long time, so I do think . . .'

Angel must have rung off, as Lady Standish suddenly went quiet and stared at her phone. She sat there in deep silence, patting the mud pack into place. I crept away, my back hunched up. There'd have to be another time for breaking in; if I dared to brave the sad asylum that seemed to be Harker Hall.

I lay on my bed with a Buddhist chillout mix on the iPod. The twang of exotic instruments . . . rootsy strumming . . . tribal breaths blowing into deep space . . .

As the music swirled I went into a trance. My brain was thick with forest greenery, Angel's white face, her mother's muddy one, flashes of their underwear, the empty farmhouse, a strange diary, and Standish's banknotes falling like dead leaves.

My bedroom door was banged. I awoke rudely into darkness. 'Samson!' Dad said. 'Samson, come downstairs. Your mother and I have something to ask you.'

I tried to sound sleepy. 'Uh? What's up? I'm kind of close to shut-eye.'

'I said, *now*! For once in your life obey somebody!'

Twenty-Eight

I put on an old and smelly T-shirt. It said FEMALE AROUSAL PATCH, and I rated it as Mum's least favourite of all my tops.

The kitchen was deathly quiet. Mum sat at the table down the far end, with Dad beside her. It was like facing a juvenile court, except one judge had floppy crimson hair, and the other stank of beer.

'Sit down,' said Dad. I slumped into a chair.

'Samson,' began my father. 'This is very hard for your mother and me to grasp. I don't know, maybe we've just not understood something, but did Lord Standish offer you twenty thousand pounds recently?'

'He did.'

'And you turned his money down?'

'I did.'

'Can we ask why?'

'Sure,' I said. 'He's gonna build expensive holiday cabins up in Appletree. Or at least he's gonna try. But not without my say-so, and I say no. That woodland is mine.'

Mum leaped up and wobbled towards me. 'It is not yours! Some stinky bit of paper, written by two old drunks, means nothing.'

'Appletree became mine at birth,' I said, leaning back. 'Let his lordship contest it in court.'

Mum turned to my dad. 'Help me out, Peter,' she said. 'Lord Standish made a very generous offer of goodwill. An offer that could save this family's business – something that some of us have worked tooth and nail for.'

'Mother!' I shouted. 'If Lord Standing Joke is so certain of his rights, why ain't he up there now bulldozing? He reckons he wants a summer house, but he's hiding something and trying to buy us off. He won't face me in court because he doesn't want publicity. How can you be so thick?'

'How dare you?' Mum clutched her chest, like an actor faking a heart attack. 'You'll take Lord Standish's money, and his holiday homes will bring in the customers this pub needs. Then you'll jolly well plan for sixth-form college and learn some proper catering skills.'

I yawned and stretched. 'I can't decide now. I'll sleep on it.'

'You'll sleep on it!' Mum's voice went wild. 'Oh, la-di-da! The King of Cumbria will sleep on it, and give his royal verdict in the morning!'

Dad gripped his hair, shaking his head. 'Stop it,' he said. 'Can't you two ever find a day's peace?'

I got up, kicking away the chair. 'I've found my own peace,' I said. 'After five years of being a reject because of her and that bloody birthday party. I'm not giving up the one place where I feel free. And I'm not letting my hazel trees go under some posh knob's concrete.'

I was woken often that night, by doors banging and the toilet flushing. From my window I saw Dad pacing around the car park, like a prisoner in some exercise yard. A full moon flooded the playground and orchards beyond. Dad smoked a cheap cigar, as if being granted a last request.

About an hour later my mother appeared, all alone, and went to the play area. She squeezed her bottom onto a swing seat and swayed like some gross child. She even sat in the sandpit, digging her toes into brown softness. I watched without pity, as if she was a lost relative on some old film reel.

I slunk downstairs next morning, ready to do battle, but Mum greeted me with a smile. OK, a smile is pushing it. Her mouth stretched and opened as if a dentist was giving the orders. 'Sit down, Samson,' she said. 'Breakfast is ready.'

I took a cautious chair to the table. Next minute I was lapping up poached eggs on toast, with grilled mush-rooms, and fresh orange juice. Dad was banging about in his workshed. Mum scoffed a platter of bacon and sausage, with fried bread. We ate in silence, me scouring the papers for more news of myself. I leafed through the dailies but the Cumbrian Phoenix story was cold.

The soaring summer heat and fears of a drought had taken over.

After we'd eaten, Mum cleared the plates, then sat beside me with some brochures and papers. With a huge effort she spoke in a polite manner. 'I just want to show you some of the things I've dreamed about. Some of the plans I had for this place. For a start, I hoped one day to have a wood-fired oven outside. There's all sorts you can do with them. Breads, real pizzas, roasted fish, proper steaks.'

Mum showed me the diagram of an oven she had in mind. I had to smile. With its beehive dome of a roof, it looked like a big charcoal mound. That's how the old burners used to pile it up in Cherry's day. The brochure said, 'You have to keep a fire going in the oven lest it cool.' And that's the same with charcoal burning too. You must keep the wood at a smoulder inside.

'We could use your charcoal to fire it up,' said Mum slyly. 'But the best brick ovens cost thousands. If you took Lord Standish's offer—'

'If I took his offer I'd be selling my soul. And if he pulls off this scam, we'd lose a huge strip of natural forest. Could you live with that?'

The grinding of teeth started. The heaving breast wheezed. 'You really have no clue,' said Mum. 'Yes, we can sell this place and clear the debts. And then what do we do? Get a house in some town and all work for McDonald's?' She threw a pile of her menus across the table. Eat the View, Eat the View . . .

Dad came in with a bottle of his new brew. 'Has he agreed? Did you tell Samson I need cash to invest in my brewery?'

'No,' said Mum. 'Has he hell agreed. A head full of daft ideals and no heart.'

I stood up and yelled. 'I'm trying to preserve something of our heritage! To save something of real value.'

'So am I!' Mum shouted, waving a menu.

'So am I!' Dad cried, shaking a bottle.

So were we all; we just couldn't see it in each other.

My mother gripped the table. 'Samson,' she said. 'Do you still refuse to take Lord Standish's money?'

'I do. To the very end.'

'Then to hell with you. And get out of this house now!'

I swept Mum's menus to the floor and ran upstairs, where I calmly packed a rucksack of clothes and stuff. Dad tried to stop me but I pushed him aside and left.

TWENTY-NINE

I unpacked my bag in Cherry's hut: a few smelly shirts, the iPod, bog rolls, and some graphic novels. I checked that my old document was still safe under the brush-wood bed.

The big snag to Cherry's hut had always been its lack of a toilet, flushing or otherwise. So I'd dug some-thing dodgy nearby once, with my billhook and trowel. A layer of ashes after every visit helped to compost it down.

Another hassle to living rough was food. I'd have to start eating the view for real, and go grubbing for fruits and nuts. I knew where summer bushes grew, laden with juicy gems. And there were always our orchards to pilfer, in night-time raids.

After crashing out in the afternoon heat I was hungry enough to go foraging. I took a Co-op bag and headed into the dim groves of beech, ash and elder. Then I strode along the top ridge of trees until they thinned out, picking blackberries. Finally, it was over a stone wall and down the mole-hilled meadows. I was close to Angel's secret squat, where the stream gasped for wetness. I followed the trickle along, wading through giant daisies and wild grasses. Over to my right were fields of golden scrub. I was about to stick on the iPod when I heard someone singing.

It was a girl's voice, pure and clear, and I guessed right off it was Angel. She sang a haunting rhyme, full of slow sweetness.

'London Bridge is falling down . . . my fair lady.'

I went onto all fours and crept forward with my face among thistles. Up ahead I got a glimpse of white skin. Somebody was bathing in the rock pool that formed where the stream came to an end. It was still deep enough to paddle in, with a circle of hard clay all around.

Her voice rose to the red and blue skies of early evening. I crawled to the foot of a huge oak tree, from where I could look down a riverbank to the pool below.

Angel was naked, her back to me, her face towards the far forests. Her white hair fell like strands of ice. There was no breath of breeze to disturb it. She hummed to herself in secret innocence, a simple child of nature again. Her hands caressed her body as she kept on humming the nursery tune. When she stretched out her arms, I saw they were criss-crossed with scratch marks. There was a sweet sadness in Angel's voice.

'Take a key and lock her up, lock her up . . . lock her up.'

She stood in her own world, like the last living soul on earth.

'Gold and silver I have none . . . I have none, I have none.'

After each verse she sat in the shallow water, and rose

again with a splash. Then she sang the rhyme once more with closed lips, droning like a bee.

I hid there and shivered with desire. Angel's bum was soft and skinny. She stood in the rock pool, and then bent over to scoop up some water. She leaned forward, as if bowing to the brook, her hands rubbing together.

Finally she faced towards me, almost like she knew I was there. I kept one eye peeking around the trunk as she bathed her front all over. Trickles of water ran down her shiny skin. A shudder ran through me as she touched her secret self. And still she hummed away as if the woods and sky were a willing audience. Her hard blue eyes stared from a solemn face. When the song rhyme was over, Angel wandered back up the dry stream towards that ruined house. I sat tight against the tree trunk, hardly breathing. My charcoals blazed.

You rotten sod.

Cherry's voice struck me like lightning. I sat up suddenly on the brushwood bed in his old hut.

'I'm sorry. I couldn't look away.'

Aye, so I saw. It's one thing to be sweet on a girl. Another to invade her private moments.

I stared out at the pitstead, where Cherry must also have spent many lonely hours. 'I'm sorry. How can I make it up?'

I waited in the drowsy woodland.

You can give her some proper love. Not with your mucky paws, but by looking after the child. You can tell she's not right. And you know why.

'It's different now. And she may not even come back to me.'

She'll find you, because she needs you. You're both mad, but together you make good sense.

I sat on a tree-stump by candlelight in the late evening. While I'd been gone earlier, Dad must have paid a visit as a bag of sarnies and drinks sat in the hut, with a note:

'Come back, Samson. Your mother didn't mean it. Let's talk things through.'

No chance. I would stick it out alone in my wood. I scoffed the food and then paid a visit to my toilet, at the edge of the clearing behind a tree. I squatted over the hole like a savage. But going back to Cherry's wigwam for a hand wash in my bucket, I heard someone scuffling at the pitstead. Thinking it was Gregson, I charged out of the trees with a roar.

Angel screamed and put a hand across her heart. 'Samson!'

'Oh, hey! I thought you were someone else.'

She was breathless with nerves and had to sit down. 'We've just got back from a craft fair. I was gonna leave you a note. The thing is, we're going away for good soon. I wanted to see you.' She stared me out.

'Oh,' I said. 'That sucks.'

'I know. For me too.' Angel was wearing a posh

blue frock and trainers, and clearly hadn't expected to find me there.

'Nice clothes,' I said.

'Thanks. I got them second hand, with some busking money.'

'Neat. You must be good buskers.'

'We are,' said Angel. 'We're a real family team.'

She came and stood beside me, lit by moonlight and candle lamps. 'Hey, have you read about this Cumbrian Phoenix? Soon there'll be real anarchy here.'

'You reckon?' I said. 'It's not just media hype?'

'No way! I wonder what he looks like.' Angel kicked off her new trainers and wandered around. 'I reckon he's pretty tall,' she said. 'And his hair is, like, dark and scruffy. And his face is kind of handsome, but has the scars of woodland battles.'

'He's a hero,' I said. 'Hey, and so are you, breaking into Harker Hall. And what you stole was dead useful, but I need something even more serious. I dunno, maybe some official letters.'

That made Angel stare again. Her eyes fixed on me like blue steel.

'I can try,' she said. 'I think the guy has some locked drawers in there. Maybe he leaves them open sometimes.'

'Whatever you can manage. Thanks.'

Angel's face hardly moved. 'I'm tired now,' she said, getting up. 'Listen, do you have a mobile?'

I'd got it switched off so my parents couldn't phone,

but I gave Angel the number. 'Didn't think you'd have one,' I said.

'Yeah,' said Angel. 'I'm a traveller, not a stone-ager.'

'I know. And you're a true anarchist.'

At this, she flung her fragile arms around me. I hugged her back, feeling my charcoals burning below. When the heat grew too intense Angel let me go and ran off.

And I stood there feeling like a Judas.

THIRTY

I awoke next morning to more bright sunshine, and Dad's worried face. 'Come home, son. We can't go on like this.'

'I can. No problem.'

Dad held out a warm parcel. 'Breakfast,' he said, sitting on a fallen branch. 'Your mother made it.'

'Not hungry.'

'Oh, for God's sake! She's your mother. You only get one, you know. When's it gonna stop?'

'Who knows? I blame her for things, she hates me for others.'

Dad's bum slid off the branch. He lay down slowly until his head was on a cushion of twigs. To my dismay he began to weep a few tears, his hands trying to cover his brown eyes. 'She's very poorly, your mother,' he said. His voice was a sorry whisper. 'She's got some heart condition . . . can hardly breathe most days, but she won't accept it. And she will run around like a mad thing. I couldn't manage life without her.'

I fell back on the sleeping bag and sticks. 'Oh, hell,' I said. And staring at the triangle of roof poles above, I noticed that years of winter rain had worn away a little skylight. The day was golden beyond this dull den.

Then a scene from my childhood exploded with sudden clarity. We were on a beach somewhere – probably Silecroft, on Cumbria's west coast. All I could recall was a stormy sea, grey waves and gusty wind. Me and Mum were taking shelter in a cave along the beach. She pointed up at the wild sky, to a small gap in the gloom. A little hole of blue, hinting at better weather to come.

'That's where the north wind lives,' said Mum. 'He'll blow away soon and go home for his tea.'

I huddled against her. 'What does the north wind have for tea?'

'He has lots of black clouds in his stew, like big dumplings. And when he's eaten them all up, the sun will come back out. You'll see.'

Was there a brief time when we were happy together? I guess there must have been, long before that birthday party when I became a scarred dropout. Before my mother's every screeched word set my brain on edge.

Dad reached for my hand and I let him grasp it. His palm was hot and sweaty, but through it I could feel his body trembling.

And so, after all that, I packed my rucksack and went home. Me and Mum made a sort of grudging peace again, and soon enough I was stuck in the piping-hot kitchen. Mum was outside taking photos of kids at play, on the swings and in the sandpit. She kept a scrapbook with pictures of visiting brats. I stood and scowled in the doorway as my mother came back.

'Why are you such a child of sorrows?' she asked.

By closing time, Dad was running a late bar for those with hollow legs. Tipsy Sid ogled the Night Clubbing pages in the *Evening Post*. He tore out the main photo: a gang of girls from Dalton posing in wet T-shirts. Then he went walking home, with the occasional hop, skip and a jump.

I was about to head upstairs when my text bleeped. It was from Angel:

I STOLE LETTERS FOR U. LOOKS WEIRD. MEET ME NOW.

She was crouched inside Cherry's hut like a scared puppy, in a flowery dress with its hem just below her knickers. When I arrived she crept out, then shrank back at a sudden clatter of blades. Through the circle of space above the pitstead we watched a small helicopter fly over, its red light flashing.

'Standish,' Angel said. 'He's made a landing site on his back lawn for that thing.'

'You're OK,' I said. 'It's too dark to be seen from up there.'

Angel sat on my twiggy bed. 'You better look at these, then I'll try and break in to put them back. There's always a window open.'

She never missed a beat, I thought. How easy was it to slip into another character like this and never mess up? At least she was still proving useful. All I had to do was keep on playing the game.

I took the papers from her and lit a lamp. They were mostly business letters, or faxes of legal notes, but I read them with growing shock.

It seemed like Lord Standish wasn't the real big shot behind this scheme. Nothing like it. From what I could make out, he had sold Appletree Wood off to the highest bidder. And now the new owner was trying to push ahead with the holiday homes before any objections were raised. Someone was putting the squeeze on Standish to act quickly. There was even a threat made against one of his other business interests.

There was no direct reference to the owners. It was all written in code, using nicknames.

'What is it?' said Angel as I read.

I put the documents down. 'Here's what I reckon. Standish bought Harker Hall, after thinking that Appletree came with it. It's called Ashburner's Wood on the original plans he saw. He knew this bit of forest would make a perfect site for log cabins and the like. So he sold it off to someone loaded, for a good profit.'

'OK,' said Angel. 'What else?'

I paced around the pitstead. 'This wood lies just inside National Park ground, which makes clearing it a risk, even if you own the land. I think somebody with more clout than Standish is turning the screw. They wanna get the ball rolling, maybe knock up a show home, and then it's too late to be stopped.'

That was the first moment I saw Angel smile; a real smile, not just a curve of cold lips. 'Turning the screw,' she said. 'That sounds good. What can I do?'

I handed her the sheets. 'Could you sneak these back? What I've read might be enough to stir up some press interest. But I still need more. Something to show who's backing all this, and how much dosh is changing hands.'

Angel put the papers aside, then carried a lump of charcoal over to me. She pushed me down, sat before me, and started colouring my face with black streaks. The slow scrape of burned wood mingled with its dark aromas. I sat there, legs out, like someone being made up for the stage. And then Angel was suddenly astride me, as my own charcoals glowed like a furnace. I stared into her blank and beautiful face. Her eyes that hardly blinked, her long white cheeks. Like mother, like daughter, I thought. I had seen that same cold sorrow in Lady Standish.

I swallowed hard. Knowing her other life made Angel seem creepy to me. She rubbed the charcoal down my neck, jabbing it against my Adam's apple. It felt more of a threat than something playful. I put a hand up to stop her.

Churrrrr . . . Jarrrrr . . . Churrr . . . Jarrr. A nightjar stabbed the silence.

'What's wrong?' Angel whispered.

'Nothing,' I said. 'Nothing's wrong.'

She whispered again, right in my ear, 'Then why do you look so scared?' Every hair on my neck stuck out like hot needles. I slowly shook my head, unable to avoid Angel's blue eyes. She touched my smears. 'I like it when you look tribal,' she said. Her voice was so soft I almost had to read her lips. Her hair was pure white in the smudgy forest.

She edged herself closer until our noses rubbed. Her small fingers began to stroke the backs of my much bigger hands. Then our lips tickled together like feathers. Angel's tongue stabbed against mine, so I grabbed the back of her head in my sudden hunger. My body tumbled hers to one side. I knelt astride her, hands rubbing her breasts for what seemed like ages. Then my face was edging down to her flat stomach, where I kissed flower prints on the white cotton.

I lifted my head and looked down at Angel. Her eyes were gazing up and away, through that break in the trees, to the starry diamonds above. Her sugar-spun hair lay on a pillow of ashes.

'Can I?' I begged. 'Can I?'

Angel tried to ease away my head, but hunger for her body fired me. I lifted her skimpy hem, my tongue and teeth tasting soft skin, as blood rippled my heart. She pushed herself back and rolled onto one side, her spine facing me. 'Not yet,' she whispered. 'I'm not ready.' When I reached out to stroke her hair she jumped up and ran, stumbling over an old beer crate.

The nightjar sang on alone. *Churrrrr . . . Jarrrrr . . . Churrrrr . . . Jarrrrr . . .*

Back in our orchard playground, I sat on the swings into the early hours. I still carried the scent of Angel, like the wolf that I was. It filled the night around me. I swayed there in a dream until I nearly slid off my seat.

I lay down in the sandpit, which was growing cold after hours of being heat-soaked. Then this dream of a dark summer's day came over me. An inky sky, a barley field, and a girl with Angel's platinum hair. She lay close by me with beads of sweat on her top lip. We tore up golden stalks and threw them away until nothing stood between us. It was neither day nor night, under such bleak clouds, but the soil below me was baking. A hot and dusty bed.

With both eyes closed, my other senses took over. I could touch the girl, and listen as she sighed. Her breath was like the whispering barley. I could smell the girl, and taste each raw secret. Her pink mouth was like spice and petals. We lay in a twilight shimmer, the breeze turning suddenly colder.

That field became the sandpit where I awoke, with a lonely ache trying to burst through. And when it finally tore me open, I let the moonlight wash me clean again.

I lay curled up like something in the womb, knowing nothing of this painful life to come.

Taking off my boots, I dug both feet into cool sand, making small burrows. Suddenly I sat up and got busy in the square pit. Working by moonlight, I formed the sand into a rough castle. First it was heaped into four long walls. And then I put little towers on each corner, and knocked a gateway through. It even made good sense to dig a moat around the front. Nobody must breach this fortress! It was built high on the highest mountain, so all my enemies could be seen from miles away.

But then in a sudden frenzy I stood up and stamped it all flat. Every turret and tower got mashed back into the dry pit. I hurled handfuls of sand at the white moon, and yelled at it.

'All I want is a chance!'

THIRTY-ONE

I slept in late but nobody came to disturb me. When I felt too het up with last night's memories to lie still, I had to do something about it.

Later, I went up the lane to a phone box on the main road. I'd noticed all the reports in the *Evening Post* on my Cumbrian Army had been written by one reporter, Eleanor Garside. I phoned their office in Barrow.

'Hello, *Evening Post*. Sarah speaking.'

I put on a deep and gruff voice. 'Is Eleanor Garside there?'

'She's not in yet. Can I help?'

An angry growl. 'This is the Cumbrian Phoenix.'

'Who, sorry?'

An even deeper growl. 'The Cumbrian Phoenix!'

'Oh, OK. Is that a local pub?'

I slammed down the phone with a curse. It was half an hour before I dared phone again, and this time I did it without the dumb voice.

'*Evening Post*, Eleanor speaking.'

'Eleanor Garside?'

'Yes.'

'This is the Cumbrian Phoenix. You should put some questions to Lord Standish, of Harker Hall in Wolf Hill. Ask him about his plans for holiday homes there. Ask him whose money is really funding the project, and why he's rushing it through. Got that?'

A patter of speedy typing. 'Yep. Got it. Can I just ask . . . ?'

I put the phone down, then wiped the handset free of fingerprints. My heart throbbed as I walked home, where Dad was chalking his daily slogan on the sign-board outside. All the funny stuff had now gone. It just said:

WELCOME TO THE FORGE

'Hey,' I said.

'Morning.' Dad sounded fed up.

'What's wrong?'

He sat on a beer barrel by the whitewashed wall. 'Your mother's ill again. I'm taking her into hospital later. They'll keep her in overnight this time.'

'Oh. Well, I'll look after things here.'

'Aye, you'll have to. Tipsy Sid's doing the bar, if he ever turns up.'

'Right. Um, did you mention to Mum what you told me? About, you know.'

'No, because the doctor told me certain things in private. Your mother doesn't want to know the real danger she's in. And I can't find the right time to tell her.'

Mum wobbled into the kitchen later, and I picked up a menu. 'Your daily specials look great,' I told her. 'I'll push them to everyone.'

'Right. Good. I should be home by tomorrow.'

'Don't rush. Let me carry those bags for you.'

'It's fine. I can manage.'

Dad was back from the hospital later, in time to brown-nose Lord Standing Joke again. Standish strolled into the front bar, ducking under its ancient door frame. I hung about in the stone-flagged passage, lit by an old iron lantern. The bar where drinks were served was so small it was strictly for boozers, not diners. That evening it was full of local farmers, just back from an auction.

Peeking inside, I saw Dad stand suddenly to attention for Standish, like some lazy soldier. 'Good evening, Lord Standish,' he said. 'Your usual, sir?'

That was a laugh. Your usual? He'd only been in once.

'Thank you, landlord. One for yourself, and I'll open a tab if I may. I'd like to treat your regulars, should they have time to hear me out.'

A murmur of thirsty thanks rippled the room. Tipsy Sid was first to drain his nearly full pint and hold it out for more, but the others weren't far behind. Farmer Wilson was there, tall and stiff, his cheeks like autumn apples. His two lads were also in, but I'd hardly spoken to them in five years.

Standish filled the doorway and addressed the room. 'Gentlemen,' he said. 'As you may know, I recently bought Harker Hall. My business has been in property development over many years, including a role on the Motorway Agency board. The original plans of Harker Hall show that its land includes Appletree Wood, which isn't owned by the Forestry Commission.'

'Aye,' said Sid. 'But the Ashburners have a claim on it. That right, Pete?'

I could sense my dad's blushes. 'Well, in a way,' he mumbled. 'Some ancient deed of my grandfather's made with old Lord Harker. Not sure it's worth the paper it's scribbled on.'

Bloody traitor.

Standish agreed with my father. 'I'm afraid it's likely to prove worthless. But what will be worth a great deal to this community are the homes I plan to build there. Attractive log cabins, hidden tastefully among the trees. All of them bringing wealthy owners, only too eager to buy local produce from you people. Perhaps you could open a collective farm shop. Gentlemen, my point is, I know times are hard for the farmer. And for the publican with a commitment to quality. What you all offer is a dream, a rural dream, and there are many out there only too eager to live it with you.'

Wot, no summer house? But he was good, I thought.

Nowt missing but a weeping orchestra.

There was a pause here while the farmers drank into Standish's money, and mulled over his Big Idea. Mr Wilson spoke up. 'Do we have your word on all this, sir? And that the plans are in good taste, like you say?'

Standish must've spouted this baloney to big public meetings before. These poor Wolf Hill clods were a pushover.

'Of course,' he said. 'As the wood is privately owned by me, I could sell it off to a developer. But I wish to oversee the whole process myself, and ensure its integrity.'

That meant the *Evening Post* had phoned him and he was desperate to get ahead.

I suddenly felt itchy about something. Leaving Standish on his soapbox, I ran up to Cherry's hut for my old deed. I would return to the pub, brandish it, and prove to them all that Standish's project could never happen.

Surely I'd left it in the tin box under my bed. It wasn't there, and yet nothing else was missing. I kicked the whole place apart for ages, throwing earth and ashes everywhere, but all to no avail. My title deed was gone.

Someone had come by and stolen it.

THIRTY-TWO

It felt like losing my name or having my ID nicked. The wood defined who and what I was. Without my paper of proof I had nothing.

There was one photocopy somewhere among my bedroom junk. But after raging through all my school papers, old comics, internet printouts, charcoal books and rock mags, it still didn't turn up. I should have made more copies but of course I hadn't. I never banked on someone grubbing through my hut to find it.

Next day after the lunch service I snuck down to Harker. I must get my document back to stake any legal claim. The hall's driveway was closed with a steel farm gate. On its left was an opening in the hedgerows to a paddock. Tall shrubs grew on the right, and gave good cover as I sneaked along. Hidden by the trunk of a great spreading oak, I spied on Harker Hall's front door as it opened suddenly.

Out came Standing Joke and the blondie twins. No Angel, although Standish called back to her, 'Victoria! We're ready.'

Angel never showed. The others all stared up the

driveway until Standish suddenly turned to the twins, and they began singing. *'Happy birthday, dear Mummmeeee! Happy birthday to yooooooo!'*

The three of them clapped and cheered as Lady Standish forced a smile. She wore a stunning aqua dress, like a swirl of pure ocean. Her slender tanned arms were bare. Her golden hair was bunched up in coils.

A flatbed lorry came crunching down the gravel drive. On the back was another vehicle, wrapped in huge sheets of pink paper. It was clearly a big motor – maybe a Jag by the shape – but covered in a layer of pure pink. On the roof was a giant red bow, tied all the way around and underneath.

Driving all this was a mechanic from the garage in Coniston. Standish had got him to deliver his wife's present, all neatly gift wrapped, and bring it right down to his front door. The driver in overalls jumped out, let down a sliding ramp, and rolled it off in front of them.

With a flourish, Standish offered his wife the key. She untied that enormous red bow then tore off the pink paper. It fell away to reveal a silver Jag. The sunlight made it look almost liquid. Standish stood close by, all smiles, and handed the garage guy some money. He thanked Standish, and reversed his lorry back out around the Jag.

'There you go, darling,' said Standish. 'Happy birthday.' He kissed her like she was an aunty. Lady Standish looked at herself in a wing mirror, stroking her cheeks, then led the twins back inside.

Her husband stayed there, patting the motor's bonnet. He was halfway to the door when his phone went. He listened hard for a minute, then replied. 'You've got the extra drill bit? Good. Get started first thing after the weekend. I'm housing the men over at Ambleside, in student halls. There's some sort of training college there. Speak soon.'

He ended the call and texted. Then he stroked the Jaguar again and went indoors.

I had picked the wrong time to sneak in, but there might not be a right one. This was Friday. On Monday it sounded like the battle would begin and I was almost out of bombshells.

My father rustled the *Evening Post*. He read out, '*Money from the house sales will be used to provide services for people in the region.*'

'Huh?' I said, leaning over the kitchen table.

'It's what Lord Standish said. Look.'

I grabbed the newspaper off him. Eleanor Garside had called Standish, but he'd charmed her away with some blarney about his private woodland, and helping the local community. I read out the end bit. '*The* Evening Post *has also made personal contact with the Cumbrian Phoenix. Since his recent threats of arson*

171

against new holiday homes, the Phoenix has gone to ground.'

My dad huffed. 'What an idiot,' he said. 'Some idler with a talent for trouble.'

Later that day, the newest branch of Standish's fan club came to bug me. I was quietly skinning some hazel branches outside Cherry's hut. Like a safari team, the Wolf Hill farmers came hacking through the bushes. They were led by Mr Wilson, big and bony, his thin hair all damp. Behind him were Cumbrian beefcakes of fattier stock. Among them was Farmer Dixon, who'd left that dead rooster on Harker Hall's doorstep. He clearly had no gripe with the Standish set now.

The two Wilson boys hung about, still wary of the misfit they'd helped create five summers ago. I nodded at Henry. 'All right?'

He gave a vague nod, rubbing his sandy hair and looking awkward.

'I'll get to the point,' said Mr Wilson. 'Whatever rights you reckon you've got to this wood, the game's over. Lord Standish can do what he chooses here, and you'll not cause a rumpus over it.'

'Aye,' said Mr Dixon. He scratched his crotch under a rolling belly. 'These new folks coming here will buy their produce direct from us. They'll get their country life dream, and we cut out the middle men. That keeps some of our transport costs down, which are bloody crippling.'

I sat and skinned hazels, but shook my head. 'Standish is using you. Why can't you see it?'

'We're not here to argue,' said Mr Wilson. 'We're the ones who live off the land, not you. Get in Standish's way, and we'll get everyone to boycott your pub.'

THIRTY-THREE

On Saturday morning I watched Henry Wilson drive a combine harvester through sun-drenched barley. No dumb kids leaped out before the blades, but I still sensed the ghosts of five summers past. I saw Blind Baxter steering wildly in the top field, with Henry yelling on the combine's footplate. Black sacks of hay tumbled in my mind.

And then one of those ghosts came riding by me, near Harker Hall's gate. Hearing hooves in the lane, I tugged on Green, Dark & Shady. The girl on the white beast was Molly Hatton. At sixteen she had lost the puppy fat of years ago, and had impressive boobs. Her long brown hair was pony-tailed, her face well tanned with farm work. I often wondered what I owed her for bringing those cylinders of hay down over me. I thought she would just ride past, but she slowed up.

'Hey,' said Molly. 'I heard about your mum. Is it serious?'

'Uh? Oh, who knows? She was in hospital overnight.'

'Right.' The horse shuffled impatiently. The combine growled like a war machine. 'What you doing next term? Your mum told mine you're doing catering.'

I kept my eyes on the red harvester, and shrugged. 'We might have sold up by then.'

'No way! There's, like, a dozen new holiday cabins coming here. They'll be worth thousands to Wolf Hill.'

'Yeah? Do you really wanna see Appletree turned into concrete?'

'It won't be,' said Molly, stroking the horse. 'They'll blend the cabins into those trees. You'll hardly notice.'

'I will. They'll destroy what's mine.'

Molly nudged the horse and it clopped on. 'It's how things are,' she said. 'It's all give and take now.'

I watched her ride away, her black jodhpurs around a lush bum. In the driveway to Harker Hall, that silver Jaguar stood like another symbol of how things were now.

I squinted at the tigerish sun. Where was my place in this world gonna be?

Dad went to fetch my mother back from hospital. They'd made her stable for now and she came home to her kitchen kingdom, ignoring Dad's pleas to take it easy. She grumbled at me for not seasoning the damson chutney, like she'd never been gone.

I was in the double doghouse. Standish was going ahead with his plans anyway, and I'd lost our chance of his money. For a final attempt to stop him, I needed my document to take to the press, or the lawyers. It was time to confront Standish about it. Or steal it back.

This time I could hardly even get down Harker's driveway. A line of trucks and diggers had rolled in there, ahead of the planned demolition of Appletree on Monday.

I weaved among yellow trucks and earth movers as the Hall's front door opened and Gregson came out with Standish. They were having angry words so I hid by a lorry in shadows.

'Someone leaked something,' said Standish. His footsteps crunched closer. 'A local reporter rang up asking who's really behind all this, and ran a story. Then the phone never stopped ringing with snoopers. Have I got a felling licence? What volume of trees will be cleared in one year? Does it include the redwood . . . Red Dwarf, or something? Did I know it was protected?'

'I assure you, sir,' said Gregson, 'that none of the men were briefed.'

Standish stopped. 'Get going first thing Monday, and I'll handle the rest. Make discreet enquiries among the men. If you sniff a rat, then sack him.'

'Will do, sir. It was probably that scruffy hippy from the pub, making trouble.'

'Father or son? They both look like scruffy hippies. The old man forced his home-brew on me the other night. If their food's that foul no wonder they're finished.'

The mobile in my pocket buzzed, blowing my cover. I flicked it off, then stepped out, trying to stay cool.

'Oi, Standish. You got my legal document?'

Standish stood with hands on hips, his brow creased. 'I really don't know what you mean,' he said. 'My goodness, has it gone missing?'

Gregson chipped in, stroking his chin. 'Now, where, oh where could it be? Have you looked in your sock drawer?'

I pulled any old piece of paper from my pocket, and waved it. 'I've got a copy. See? But I want what's mine.'

The two men walked on, inspecting their machines like war generals. I went after them but my mobile rang again, showing Angel's number, so I wandered into the bushes. I felt weird answering it, knowing she might only be yards away. She might even be watching.

'Hey,' I said softly.

'Hey, Samson. Where are you?'

'Oh, just dossing around.'

'Right. Listen, can you meet me tonight? About half twelve?'

'Why so late?'

'You'll see. On the road above Wolf Hill, by the signpost. We're moving on soon, the caravan's nearly ready.'

'Hell. Listen, I know it's a big ask. Standish stole my title deed to Appletree. Any chance you could sneak in and see if it's lying about?'

'I'll give it a go. See you later then?'

'OK.'

I ran back up the drive, looking to find Standish again. But he and Gregson were crossing the fields towards Wilson's farm, and I wouldn't reach them now, or even know what to do if I could.

THIRTY-FOUR

I looked at my watch and went quickly up the lane. It was after half twelve. Angel was near the hedgerow by the hidden sign pointing back down to Wolf Hill. She wore a red top with a Communist star, a khaki jacket, a short denim skirt and boots. She looked every inch the rich rebel.

I felt a bit spooked, as we hadn't met up since I tried it on with her in the wood. She stared back without feeling.

'Hi,' I said. 'What's new?'

'This.' She whipped out her mobile and held it to my ear. I heard a recorded message. *'High Pressure sound system collective. DJ Conscious Pilot speaking. Copper Mines Valley . . . Coniston . . . one a.m. Over.'*

Angel smiled. 'It's a free party. And we're going.'

'You're kidding.'

'No. Look, we can thumb a lift. There'll be loads of ravers heading that way.'

I wasn't ready for this, and wanted Green, Dark & Shady, but Angel cared nothing for that. 'Come on, Samson. It'll be awesome. I bet the Cumbrian Phoenix is there. You can tell him about your plans for Appletree.'

I tagged along behind on the gloomy road. I had met

Angel in the hope of getting my document back. 'No luck there,' she said.

'Right. The heavy machines move in on Monday. If there's anything you can get for me before then . . .'

Angel was almost a shadow shape. 'I'll try,' she said. 'Keep your phone on tomorrow and wait.'

We headed downhill for the main route between Broughton and Torver. The forest on our left stirred with its own night life. The narrow tips of conifers were like church spires in the dark. At last we came to level ground, and a road heading north to Coniston, or south to the sea.

Angel stood in the road, her thumb aloft. A few cars whizzed past, lurching with drunken drivers who thought they were safe out in the sticks. Before long a white van came by, its stereo pumping an earthy mix of drum 'n' bass. As it pulled to a halt, Angel turned to me. 'Just do what I do, OK? Don't mess up.'

We got in the back, which was full of people, the air thick with herbal smoke. As we pulled away, someone shouted, 'You guys know where the free party is?'

'Yeah,' I said. 'I know Copper Mines.'

That got me some respect, and a bottle of organic cider. Sitting across from me was a girl. Her face was a bit oriental, a bit brown. Her eyes were large with heavy lids. She had a mole above her top lip, with a tiny thorn of hair growing from it. I imagined kissing her and feeling that mole in my mouth.

'I'm Asha,' she said.

'Samson,' I replied.

'Simpson?'

'No, Samson. Like the Bible guy who pushed over those pillars.'

'Cool. The one whose hair got shaved by Delilah.'

'The same. Only my locks ain't for cutting.'

Asha smiled. She had long brown hair with coloured threads woven in. Her eyebrows were thick and curly like caterpillars. She wore a white top splashed with pink patterns. Angel sat beside me, staring at Asha and drinking. The air was heavy with smoke and bass beats as the van rattled on towards Coniston.

Through the back window I saw a stream of headlights behind. We were leading more vehicles in the party pack. Coniston village was normally dead to the world after midnight, but now it was being invaded.

'Over the crossroads,' I said as the music dimmed. 'Past the garage on your right, then turn left. Now take that steep lane between the pub and the Co-op.'

There were ten others in the back, crammed toe to toe. They sat in silence as the van twisted up by meadows and cottages.

'There's a cattle grid on the left,' I said. 'Go across it, then veer right along the track. It's a rough ride.'

Copper Mines Valley was wide, stony and got boggy in winter. But that summer, great cracks had opened in the earth, wide enough to jump over. In the headlights, sheep scattered to the fells as we drove along a bumpy road. Rising before us were lumpy triangles of mountain. Their lower slopes and surrounding hills marked the valley's edges.

The van parked up and everyone piled out to breathe country air. Hidden in the shadow of trees was another large gang who broke from cover like an army.

The word was that a sound system from Preston, down the motorway in Lancashire, was approaching. They played dub, reggae, drum 'n' bass and jungle at free parties and squats, and in their own nightclub.

'Any chance of the cop shop showing?' Angel asked.

'None,' said Asha. 'The later you set up, the less likely you'll get caught. Easier to shut down a party that hasn't started than one with two hundred ravers.' Her narrow brown eyes met mine. Her face was heart-shaped, with tribal pink lips. I stared at her mouth and its mole.

The party animals chattered like manic insects as a dark truck came up the track. We jumped out of the way as more vans and cars approached, crammed with bodies. Everyone followed on their trail, like modern kids after the techno Pied Piper. The vehicles wobbled, swerving to avoid ruptures in the baked earth.

Abandoned mine works lay all around in spooky silhouette. Old gunpowder stores in ruins, water wheels, bronze wagons and crumbling towers.

There was a rising trail to the left, at the base of the mountains. We all followed the trucks up it, and passed a concrete power station on a level plateau. Then we crossed a cattle grid on the way up towards Bursting Stone quarry. People were blowing shrill whistles and waving glo-sticks in the summery dark.

'Neat place,' said Angel. 'Remote enough to keep out snoopers.'

The main truck was in position, up in the throne-shaped quarry. Bursting Stone had been hacked out of the hills down the decades, and was still working. It climbed in three horseshoe arcs, like giant steps. These were the cutting floors, where they broke down chunks of slate. Steep clay cliffs rose on either side. They enclosed the three cutting floors, with one big level at the top.

This was to be the site of my first free party. I danced for joy, raising my hands to the mountains around.

Thirty-Five

I liked Bursting Stone quarry. It was a raw rupture of life, among all those gooey pictures of Coniston the tourists are fed on.

Normally you could hear the echo of your voice or hand-clap in Bursting Stone. It was like some mountain temple, striped with bronze earth. But that night there was only music and mayhem.

I looked at its monumental back wall, as flinty as hell. The top cutting floor, the widest, was used for the main rave. The lowest was like a chillout zone. Psychedelic drapes were hung across old copper mine entrances in the hills.

The main rig was housed in the back of a truck, with bass bins throbbing. The other system was wired to a generator from a van.

I sipped a bottle of cider and wandered around. Girls of crushing beauty danced, waved arms, applauded. They went topless, braless, even skirtless.

Someone shouted over the throbbing noise, 'Samson! Up here!'

It was Asha, dancing on a yellow dumptruck, wearing a workman's hard hat. A spotlight landed on her long hair and the pendant glinting around her neck.

The sound crew had rigged up a movie projector. On the cliff face that formed the quarry's back wall, scenes from *March of the Penguins* beamed out. I felt half stoned, watching black-and-white seabirds waddle over an ancient Cumbrian landscape. Flashing lights mixed with images of a polar winter, and melting glaciers.

The hot smell of spliff was everywhere, like dark soil after rain. I saw Angel wander into the hubbub, climbing upwards on a jagged path around the three cutting floors. She touched the faces of male strangers, hugging anyone within reach. Then she disappeared among the crowd at the top, where lights washed over whirling bodies. I sat in the chill zone at the bottom, swaying to dubby rhythms and what sounded like a didgeridoo. Then I saw some crusty geezer playing one, blowing down this long wooden pipe. He was wearing only a loincloth. I sat and listened.

Asha appeared beside me later. 'I'm getting baked,' she sighed.

'Been smoking?' I asked.

She nodded. 'That Angel's getting faded too.'

'What on?'

'This,' said Asha, holding a dying spliff. 'Want some?'

'No,' I said, and left Asha to flop. I trekked up that path to the top level, where break-beats throbbed and bodies bounced under moonlight and spotlight.

I saw Angel sitting by a campfire on the grass

ridge above the quarry. Some guy next to her started skinning up, his head leaning on hers. He wore an army jacket, and had crewcut hair. Angel pulled his face towards hers and their mouths met.

I picked up a handful of gravel pebbles and flung them towards her. Maybe a few bits pelted her shoulders before I turned away into the crowd.

My last traces of feeling for Angel drained away. I had known for long enough that there would never be a me-and-her, but it still left me bitter. Only in our desperate minds had she been the wild gypsy of both our dreams.

I had to be where other people weren't, so I sneaked under a drape and into one of the mountain's mine entrances, a relic from centuries ago. The dank tunnel was cold and clammy after the frantic scenes. The further I went in, the louder grew the dripping of water. These ancient drops mingled with techno-pagan sounds from Bursting Stone, so that for a moment I stood between two worlds.

The natural echoes inside that old shaft were haunting. My soft steps bounced back at me from somewhere ahead, like I was following a stranger.

I stumbled on something metallic. The floor still had its old rails for horse-drawn wagons. Little kids half my age once lived and died down here, mining for a handful of copper.

I breathed darkness and dust, taking a leak against the rocky enclosure. Something furry and animal brushed my legs. I stifled a scream and warm wazz spattered both my trainers. Slapping blindly at cold walls, I turned and blundered back.

The trancey tunes from the lowest level guided me in. I got the pulse of random lights behind a dark drape and emerged with sweat cooling on me. On the cinema-screen cliff, a leopard seal bared its teeth like an ocean thug.

DJ Conscious Pilot announced himself from the cutting floor above. He was an older bloke in a sleeveless bomber jacket, long pink shirt, dark trousers and sandals. His sunglasses were pushed up below greying dreads.

As he spun some jungle-folk tunes, I had an idea. I pushed through the masses to his record deck and wrote a message to show him. He read it, then nodded and held up a hand to indicate five minutes.

Sure enough, after the next tune, the DJ made an announcement. 'Listen up, people! There's word here from the Cumbrian Phoenix. You've all to head for Appletree Wood in Wolf Hill on Monday morning. It's a village nearby, where a charcoal wood is being destroyed for holiday homes.'

This was met by much blowing of whistles, jeers and cheers from the crowd. I got gooseflesh at the loud reaction and joined in the noise.

A tap on my shoulder. I spun round to see Angel staring.

'What?' I said loudly.

Angel put her mouth to my ear. 'So it was you. The

Phoenix.' She stood back and ran both hands over her cheeks. I gave a modest shrug.

Angel's white face bowed as her tears began dribbling. 'God, what have I done? I'm feeling bad, really bad. Take me out of here before I die.'

We blundered down the skanky trail away from Bursting Stone, to a row of slag heaps made from crumbled copper waste. Angel gripped my arm like I was her prisoner, taking nervous glances behind. She carried a pack of lager cans.

'There's someone following,' she said.

'There's no one,' I assured her.

'There is, Samson. Let's hurry.'

'Slow down,' I said, stumbling in potholes. 'You're getting wild on that weed.'

She held me tight, but stopped once to rest her cheek on my shoulder. 'I'm sorry,' she said. 'I'm so sorry.'

'Take it easy. Let's get you sat down.'

It was after three o'clock, and some blue hints of dawn broke the sparkly night above. Our trail met the surface of the longest slag heap, and I helped Angel across it.

It was a rolling level of scabby cinders, but Angel cuddled close and I put an arm around her. It felt like I was the only familiar thing left to her.

'Samson! Who's over there? Look behind.'

I didn't need to look but did anyway. 'It's nothing, Angel, just a shadow. Calm down, you're tripping.'

Back up to my right, *March of the Penguins* was on a

rerun. Images of the Southern Lights were dancing in cosmic swirls. The penguins below stood huddled in a black mass, like little monks.

'Just hang onto me,' I said.

'I can't!' Angel covered her face and really cried this time, her trembling body racked with tension. As I held her, I felt judders in my own bones from the shudders in hers. When at last Angel could speak without blubbing, she said, 'He'll kill me. If he finds out what I've done. So will you.'

She had forgotten her secret life for once, under the full-on effects of that hash. I rocked her gently. 'Why would I kill you?' I wanted her to own up.

Angel licked her dry lips. 'You'll see,' she said, grabbing one of her cans. 'I need a drink.'

'Not that stuff. Let's get some water.'

'No.' She glugged until lager frothed back down her salty chin.

'Easy,' I said, wrestling it away. 'You'll have a seizure. It's getting lighter now: they'll be packing up here soon.'

'Stay,' she pleaded. 'Let's stay a bit.' She lay back on the tough scree, taking off her trainers for a pillow. I set my own pair down the same way. We lay next to each other, listening to the throbbing music fade, and heard the first chirping birds who'd returned after the mayhem. I could almost feel the chaos in Angel's head as it rested against mine, and she mumbled in a sleepy panic.

More patches of the universe were shading from black to blue. Now only the trancey chill zone was playing up in Bursting Stone. I closed my eyes, and felt a great stirring inside me for the healing beauty of music.

I dozed for about an hour, and when I awoke Angel was necking another can. The sky was lighter now, turning grey-white. Feedback whistled from the bass bins up in Bursting Stone, and people were straggling downhill. Several ravers had crashed out among the bracken, some in sleeping bags. Others were going around with bin liners, picking up all the rubbish and empty cans.

'Let's scoot,' I said. 'Hey, enough now.' I took the tin from Angel's lips as she coughed up warm lager. I dragged her away from the slag heap, scrabbling down the slope and onto the valley's parched floor. We jumped over slashes in the ground as if an earthquake had passed.

Then came a bridge above a trickling waterfall, where the plunging trail divided. To our left the way was full of vehicles, rolling back down to the cattle grid and road, so we crossed the bridge and took another track. It was narrow and sprinkled with rocks.

I tried slowing Angel as she turned in terror. 'Let's run,' she urged. 'C'mon, they're closer.'

She let go of my hand and rushed on, but the down-hill path lay strewn with danger. Seeing only imaginary strangers behind, Angel ran into a razor-edged rock. The impact flung her forward onto more hard slabs. She howled with shock and fright, and lay there as lambs watched from the bank above.

'I can't go on,' she whined.

'You have to.' I shook her shoulder. 'Angel, don't drop off. Please.'

When I tried to sit her straight, she went all limp and floppy. A cocktail of excess and exhaustion had shattered her. She shrieked awake when I pressed her ankle. 'It hurts!'

Angel lay down again, too tired to try. But I was double her weight, and lifted her onto my shoulders, her thighs pressed against my head. Then I slowly stood straight, bending both knees and feeling my spine ache.

I gripped Angel's legs, her slim body-weight over-head. Her short denim skirt was bunched behind my neck. Inching forward, I was thankful for a brighter sky and each footstep was a victory. Left foot . . . hold . . . right foot . . . hold . . . steady again. Then came a down-ward slab of concrete; the old wagon road leading up to Bursting Stone.

But as we reached it, Angel began to sway and pull me backwards. She must have dozed off for a moment. Then I felt something wet on the back of my neck. I knew in a flash what it was, because I'd got the same urge myself.

'Angel!' I shouted. 'Hell, you're peeing on me! Get down!'

I slapped her left thigh, kneeling quickly, and cracked my knees on cement. Angel woke at my yelling, with a sudden awareness, and clambered off. She grabbed her crotch, and waddled away almost doubled up.

I heard her knickers come down with a sense of calm, like she was a kiddy cousin caught short at the seaside. I heard a spurting on the green bank, and stared at the final starlight, feeling like I'd lived four years in four hours. The collar of my shirt was damp.

Angel did herself up, then hobbled back over like a helpless puppy. Her legs were stained with blood and wee. She couldn't even look at me.

THIRTY-SIX

I helped her down the old wagon trail, then through pastures dotted with sheep, and out onto a road where a yapping dog broke the peace. Angel leaned on me all the way down, limping and crying. We stood on a pavement near some houses at the edge of Coniston. This time I was the one thumbing a lift, but the first few cars going by were chocka. Angel clamped my hand over her breast to feel her heartbeat, where an overload of substances was kicking in.

After half an hour we got picked up by the same van again. Everyone was crashed out apart from Asha, who was up for talking. 'I'll be at Wolf Hill on Monday,' she said. 'Are you there for the protest?'

'Sure,' I said. 'It's where I live.'

She twisted a blue-pink thread in her hair. We chatted on until Asha gave a sleepy smile and closed her heavy lids.

I asked the driver to take a detour through to Wolf Hill, and he dropped us off outside The Forge, where I shook Angel awake. I wanted to see her home safely, even if that meant going to Harker

Hall. But the sight of somewhere familiar brought her senses back and she slipped into her other life. 'I'll be OK,' she said. 'I told my parents about tonight. The squat's not far.'

'Well, if you're sure. And . . . any chance of nabbing that document? It's my last chance.'

'I'll try. I owe you.' Angel turned and limped away. My brain was buzzing with music and fatigue, but I followed her downhill at a distance. From a corner hedge I watched until she turned safely along the drive to Harker Hall.

The endless hot weather seemed ready to break. Sunday lunchtime found Wolf Hill surrounded by warm and moist air. Distant thunder rumbled as if mountains somewhere might be collapsing.

It wasn't a day for hiking or sandcastles, so we had a decent turnout. My dad stood near his workshed, looking skywards. 'Here comes the flood,' he said. The Forge lay under an eerie light. Somewhere in the grim sky was a summer sun, giving each dark cloud a golden streak.

Mum lit candles inside the pub and turned the fake gas lamps on. People sat around in shirts and shorts, reading the Sunday papers.

Dad was pleading with Mum to take it easy. She ignored him, desperate for each customer to 'Eat the View' and go home happy. And her Cumberland pork and apple loaf went down a treat. Not expecting a big crowd, Mum went into overdrive trying to make enough of everything. As always I bore the brunt of her temper.

'Samson! Is that your idea of a green salad? Are you colour blind?'

'Samson! They're called mushy peas for a reason! So mush them!'

'Samson! Call that a sticky toffee sauce? It wouldn't stick to my shoe!'

Her whale of a body barged around. When I kept checking my mobile for anything from Angel, she tore it from me and put it in the freezer. At last, when the rush was over, I went upstairs and tried to call Angel. For an hour there was no reply as I sweated.

In desperation I finally went down to Harker Hall and lurked by the gateway. Anything was better than just waiting around. The sky was overcast. Then finally Angel phoned me and whispered, 'No chance to break in yet.'

'Hell.' I shrank against a tall shrub, wondering how close by she was. 'Keep trying, yeah?'

There was a long pause. I heard Angel breathe slowly through her nose, like she was asleep on my shoulder. Then a Mountain Rescue helicopter clunked over suddenly, so I had to cover my ear.

'Noisy sod,' I said. 'It's right above you. Must be rattling Harker's roof off.' And I bit down on my stupid tongue. For a second I'd forgotten the rules, and maybe given away everything.

A worrying silence followed, broken only by Angel's breaths. 'You OK?' I said. 'Lost the signal?'

'Stay by your phone,' said Angel. And she rang off quickly. I punched my chin and swore, kicking myself all the way home. Now it was a waiting game. Which half of Angel was gonna show?

Hunger drove me home, where I made a meal of leftover Cumberland loaf and cold veg. Dad came into the kitchen with a pint and sat down. 'That's it, then,' he said.

'What's what?' I mumbled, mouth full.

'That's it, we're done. Tomorrow I have to go to the estate agent and put this place on the market. We needed a lunchtime like today every day this summer to pull through. I've been praying for bad weather really. When it's so hot, everyone heads off to the tourist traps, to trough cheap ice cream, grill themselves by a lake, and kick drunken hell out of each other.'

'Bit harsh, Dad. What about all the friendly hikers and nature types?'

Dad held his pint to the light. 'Sure. Not enough find their way out here though. Wash the pots, son. Your mum needs a rest.'

I did as he asked, feeling a block of guilt in my guts.

Standish's money might have bought us another year, maybe more. I slunk upstairs to wait for a call, and lay on my bed as the clock ticked on to half past six. But lack of sleep from last night caught me up, and soon I was dead to the darkening world.

The low clouds gave a sudden clatter. I woke up in shadows, all at sea, and slapped on a light. It was nine o'clock and I checked my phone but nobody had called. The roof rattled under another storm warning.

I went outside into an air of unreal stillness. The skyline was black and deep blue.

In a cold sweat I stood and looked west over the valley. Yellow glows came from farmhouses getting ready to batten down for the night. Sheep huddled by drystone walls, as if they knew what wrath was coming. Ahead on the skyline, Stickle Pike was shrouded in grey vapours.

I took a few steps downhill, steeling myself to storm into Harker Hall and do something drastic. That's when my mobile beeped. 'Angel!' I shouted into it. 'Anything happened?'

A strange crackle echoed down the phone. It was like the static from an old radio. I waited ages for a reply. 'I've got what you need,' said Angel. She sounded calm and cold. 'I've got it all.'

'You beauty!' The noise around her piled up.

'What's happening, where are you?' More crackling waves came over the air.

'I'm at your charcoal hut,' said Angel. 'Your forest is on fire all around me. Listen to it burn, you lying bastard.'

THIRTY-SEVEN

Angel must have held out her phone, as the sparking sound grew louder. I was away down the lane like a hellcat. Hurtling past the ivy cottage, I hit the old bridleway. For a second I stopped and took in the unreal scene.

The left edge of Appletree was up ahead. Its ridge of woodland spread away to my right. The trees were in blackness, except for a red glow at the centre near my pitstead. It pulsed like a heart, sending out smoke through that break in the clearing.

I ran blindly towards it along a path I'd taken many times. Branches spat back and scratched me, as if the forest was alive with wild cats. As I drew nearer my face took the heat, like I'd opened an oven. Fire was ripping through the ferns and bracken, but the path to Cherry's hut was only warm. It led me into the clearing, where there was nothing for fire to feed on. A choking smell of petrol was everywhere.

Angel stood there in a white dress. She held a brown leather briefcase, like she was ready for a meeting. Her white face glowed as she shouted into her phone.

'Yes, Daddy, I'm in the wood. Yes, I've got your plans. Yes, they're going up in smoke.'

She shook open the case and took out some papers, then backed off and held them over burning grass.

'When did you find out?' she screamed. 'When did you start using me?'

'Angel . . . Please!' I begged her. 'I didn't always know. Not at first.'

She wafted the papers. 'It's all here. Everything you wanted.'

'Forget that. Just run.'

'No,' said Angel. 'I've nothing to go back to.' She shouted into her phone again, 'Did you hear that? Nothing to come back to!'

Thunder slammed out of the clouds like a field gun. Angel flung the papers, but a stiff wind sent them flying towards me. I scrabbled around like a beggar to gather them. Flicking quickly, I found my old title deed there. I grabbed it, along with several other documents. One of Standish's business cards went into my pocket.

Angel tried to kick the papers from my hands. She screamed more abuse at her father, who must be glued to his own phone in shock. Her body seemed to swell with anger. Her face glowed pink, red and yellow like the changing flames.

I felt a fresh wave of heat. Cherry's hut was alight,

its wigwam structure burning from the top. That's when I stuffed the papers down my pants, tore off my shirt and whipped it against the fire. It came back scorched and smoked. I even threw handfuls of earth around but nothing so flimsy could dampen the blaze.

I grabbed Angel's hand and tried to flee, but she pulled away, walking backwards, as if tempting me into hell with her. She tucked herself into a corner of Cherry's burning hut, resisting my efforts to haul her out.

That's when I lost it. Fury got the better of me. I yanked Angel back towards the pitstead, though she dragged her feet and howled. One of her fists was tight around her phone.

Fire was raging from tree to tree, in a chain reaction. The pathway back from Cherry's hut was now engulfed. Flames linked up across it. Maybe a rat could tunnel under them, but not a brawny youth like me.

The wooden frame of Cherry's wigwam began to collapse. Old slabs of muddy clay fell from the sides, like slates off a roof.

Another clatter came from on high, even louder than before. A light cut down through the gap among the trees, where smoke was being cut to shreds by an increasing wind. It searched out me and Angel, like we were criminals on the run. I stared up as if an alien craft was calling. It was a commercial light helicopter and must be Standish's.

Then, out of the swirling light above, came a long rope. It dangled like a giant string for cats to play with.

I lost all senses except for my vision. I stood in a cold vacuum, as if my life was shutting down. There was nothing to do but act. I picked up my smoky T-shirt and put it on. Angel was at her father's throat again, down the phone.

All I knew was the lifeline of that dangling rope. I tied a strong loop on its end, big enough to get a foot in. Like an old sailor, my fingers worked the thick twine. I made a noose near the ground. When I reached out for Angel, she pulled away. But my grip was too strong and she couldn't run. What she could do was fight back and waste precious seconds as the blaze got worse. She dropped her phone, to claw at my face and hair. High above, someone jiggled the rope about, testing its weight in case we were ready.

Angel aimed a knee at my groin. And that's when I hit her. A massive blow to the temple. I felt nothing as my fist struck the weak point of her skull. All I saw was her stunned eyes meet mine, then go blank as her legs gave way. She fell on my pitstead, her dress black with smoke.

I picked up her phone. If someone was yelling down

it, I couldn't hear them. So I shouted into it, my voice like an echo. 'Standish! Can you hear me? Count to thirty, then get pulling.'

My right foot went into the loop. I twisted more of the slack rope around my leg for an extra grip. It was easy to pick up Angel. She was half my weight and so much smaller. Her eyelids flickered like someone in deep sleep, and she tried pushing me. I cracked her another to make sure, and she went limp again. It was either that or leave her to die. With my hands under her armpits, I got her standing, my foot in the rope to hold steady.

It worked best to grab Angel around her waist with my left arm. I pulled more of the rope down, wrapping it across her shoulders. I draped her arms around my neck. We waited in a bear-hug embrace.

Only when the rope went stiff, and we began to rise, did my senses return to hear the hard crackling, to feel the urgent heat and thumps of terror in my head.

We rose through the smoke into a hot breeze. My pants were stuffed with documents and papers. As we climbed above the height of burning trees, the light still shone over me and Angel. Someone inside the chopper held it steady. But they could see no briefcase, only a boy and girl bound together. Angel stirred and groaned.

The helicopter blades chopped at the smoky night. It could have been my one chance to look over the woodland, but my whole being had this single focus. I must not move a muscle. I must cling to my burden. I must not look down. I must be stronger than Stickle Pike mountain, and just keep holding on.

THIRTY-EIGHT

Adrenalin hit my veins like a power surge. Angel was still limp. My right leg began to shake with strain, pressing down in the loop to stay steady. The helicopter kept treading the air, then I felt a terrible lurch as it began to fly off in the rising wind. But there was still no rain, no thunder and lightning. It was like the storm had passed over Wolf Hill without breaking, like a bully showing off.

Every nerve and muscle in me screamed with the effort. The rope was tough and scratchy in my right hand. It dug into my leg and back like I was being flayed. My fingers clawed into Angel's flesh and bones to hold her with me, the two of us lashed together.

When we cleared Appletree Wood, the helicopter dipped. I thought they might lower us into the barley field, but the landing pad behind Harker Hall was only seconds away. Standish would be up in the chopper giving orders, maybe knowing his daughter was injured, or fearing she'd been scarred in the fire.

We swooped through the darkness, Angel's dress flapping like a white flag. I squeezed my eyes closed, and let the swirls in my stomach guide me like a fairground ride. When I opened them I looked into Angel's blue ones. She had come to, totally terrified, and tightened her grip around me. Our faces bumped as the rope twisted and creaked. She stared at me in frightened silence. She never twitched, or made as if to jump, but nor did I relax my hold. An evil swelling was coming up on her temple.

We dipped to the height of a rooftop above the meadows. As we cleared the archway by Harker Hall, the chopper hovered to lower us on the lawn. The second we hit the ground I rolled over and let go of Angel. Lady Standish was waiting and ran to her daughter. I legged it home, desperate to pee, tumbling over my wild feet in the dark, as a siren wailed its way into Wolf Hill. A fat splat of rain hit my hair, and I was glad of it. Running up the lane to The Forge, I was pelted by more great drops.

I locked the door of my room, and lay on my bed in a daze.

I listened as the night really began to chuck it down. It finally rained with all the pent-up fury of a long dry summer. My dad hammered the door and barged in. 'Appletree Wood is on fire!'

I was too tired to move. 'I know, Dad. But the rain's here now.'

He touched my forehead. 'Are you ill? What the hell's going on?'

'Nothing's going on.'

Dad shook his head. 'The fire brigade's come from Coniston. Maybe you can help.'

'Sure. I'll be down soon.'

Dad left me alone and I got busy. Out came those documents from my undies, and straight into one of the box files in our office. I hid it under some games in my cupboard. There'd be time enough to read each page in detail.

Minutes later I was back outdoors, and watching the unreal drama. Two fire engines were parked in the lane, close to Harker Hall's driveway, being machine-gunned by sweeping rain. Firemen in yellow hats charged towards the barley field, their hoses feeding out like entrails. The flames in Appletree Wood absorbed every inch of the downpour. The flood began to damp down the forest fire, like the water I poured into my charcoal stacks to cool them.

Rain blobs made rivers down my face. I looked on as the fire-fighters stood back from the fire, and sprayed jets of water over the treetops. The blaze had cooked the heart of my wood, but even if it ate the entire plantation it could go no further. Sheep fields, drystone walls, fire breaks in the grasses and rocky mountain slopes would thwart it.

I hardly noticed Mark and Henry Wilson turn up to watch. Henry edged over to me by the wire fence as Appletree steamed like a rainforest. He was tall and muscular, wearing a raincoat and wellies. His younger brother stood apart, watching the buzz around the two fire engines.

'God,' said Henry. 'I hope they save your wood.'

By midnight, a thick and sour smoke lay over the mass of trees. Dad found me, and we stood together, watching on. The storm clouds, and Coniston's part-time firemen, had drenched the place. When it was obvious there was no risk, we walked home.

We dried off back in the pub, and Dad was full of questions. He said, 'What does it mean for Appletree? Where was Lord Standish tonight?'

'Busy,' I said. 'A man like that. Always busy.' I was too shattered to tell him the whole story.

At last, when he'd gone to bed, I sorted through the papers that Angel had stolen. And there it all was, set out on sheets of bank account transfers. Every bribe and backhander paid to those in authority. The names of people inside important organizations, who were taking money to let developers run riot. The ones with great power to decide what happened in obscure places like Wolf Hill. The ones who were meant to keep out the planners were the very ones who would let them in.

There were outlines of more magazine adverts, like the first one Angel got for me. Other sites were being lined up in various regions. And big money was involved if the figures I read were for real.

It was harder to work out who was squeezing Lord Standish, but I could make a guess. Someone with powerful business and government contacts, whose role in all this should have been shredded out of sight, not left on coded documents in locked drawers.

I had never felt much loyalty to Cumbria, on account of my tormented life at home and school. Nothing beyond Appletree and my charcoal site had seemed worth saving. Now I was churning with a new rage, but I suddenly went fuzzy with tiredness and fell asleep in my smoky clothes.

The rain blew itself out by early morning. Then I got myself going, scoffed some cereal, and headed up to Appletree. The woodland was still smoking like the night after a giant bonfire. Many of the trees were unharmed, but most around the pitstead were badly scorched. A lot of my skinny hazels had succumbed to the flames, but I'd enough green shoots left elsewhere to start over. Swathes of bracken and wild grasses had been razed, although their debris would enrich the soil.

I got a little fire going by what was left of Cherry's hut. Its frame had been burned, but parts of the lower mud structure remained. There were black tree stumps and ruined branches everywhere. The fire brigade had sealed off the area, but I pushed through their tape. I sat in the clearing on a warm stump, and waited for anyone to come to me.

*

I didn't wait long. Within an hour, the first footsteps crackled through and brought Standish. He looked a shattered man, with his bristles and creased shirt. He stared down on me through filters of grey smoke.

I said, 'I have copies of everything.'

Standish took a cheque from his pocket and handed it over. It was made out in my dad's name to the tune of twenty thousand pounds. The sum he'd once offered us.

'If a word of this ever leaks out,' said Standish, 'I will find some way to destroy you. Take this as a donation, to support your family's business.'

I took the cheque from him, and slid it down my kecks. Standish stood his ground. 'So, I'll have those documents off you,' he said. I held out empty palms to him. Standish almost laughed. 'Twenty grand not enough?'

'Nope. The money's fine.'

'So what else?'

'I'll let you know. Just never come back here with your plans. And if you ever harm your daughter I'll find out.'

'My daughter has never wanted for anything,' said Standish. 'At least I never used her in the shameful way that you did.'

I sat on a wobbly beer crate. 'You forget that I saved her.'

Standish dragged both hands down his cheeks,

making him look years older. 'You do realize she's the one who stole your document? She was trying to get me on her side, to change my plans about her future. Now can you see how ill she really is?'

Thirty-Nine

My parents danced like bears around the kitchen when I showed them the cheque. I left out most of the detail, but I said that Lord Standish's daughter had started the forest fire, and that this was payment for damage to Appletree.

'Amazing!' Dad said. 'But what about those holiday cabins?'

I shrugged it off. 'Not all deals go through. A window of opportunity opens, then it closes. Maybe he couldn't raise the right backers for it.'

My parents sat and shook their heads in wonder, the poor boobies. I left Dad to tell the farmers, although he made great play of Standish's kindness. 'It's bought us two years to turn things around. Drinks on the house tonight.'

'And what about Lord Standish?' Farmer Wilson asked, later in the bar. 'Is he staying on here?'

'Don't know,' said Dad. He looked at me as if I held the answer. I shook my head vaguely, clearing away empty glasses.

My mother's lack of gratitude soon began to bug me. She said, 'Thank heavens for Lord Standish. I guess he knows what it's like to have a wayward child.'

I could hardly tell her the truth, but she kept warbling on. 'You didn't throw his cheque back this time.'

'His mad family tried to burn my wood,' I said. 'But they didn't succeed, and I've already started work on the damage. Could take me months, so maybe you can afford some kitchen staff while I save the local environment.'

Mum sniffed and panted as she peeled spuds. 'If we're staying put for now, Samson, what about sixth-form college?'

'I've other plans.'

'Really. Pass my tablets. And put some more fresheners in the men's urinal.'

Instead, I went upstairs and made sure my copies of Standish's documents were safely stashed. Then I put a call through to the heritage fund, as they still hadn't replied to my proposal. I told them about last night's fire, and asked if it might affect things for me. A lady with a soft Scottish accent took my call. 'There's a letter going out to you,' she said. 'It has the details of our decision.'

'Can't you tell me more?'

'I'm not allowed to discuss cases on the phone. It should be there before too long.'

I spent my time in Appletree Wood, trimming burned branches and clearing the remains of ruined plant life.

Harker Hall looked empty, although cars still came and went. The helicopter clattered about now and then, but neither Angel nor the twins were to be seen. She never tried to contact me, and I didn't dare go near the house. Nothing I'd seen or heard in that place made me glad about the human condition.

Dad took me into his workshed one night for another tasting. I braced myself for the worst as he passed me a glass.

I took a sip, then a long slurp, and spat the whole lot out in shock. 'Flipping heck, Dad!'

'What? No good?'

'You're joking, man. It's awesome. I could neck this all night.' It was true, and I was made up for my father. He'd turned out a really cool summer beer, with a right tangy taste. 'Write it all down,' I said. 'However you did this, make sure it's not forgotten.' And we stayed up late that night getting every last detail nailed down.

The *Evening Post* came to take photos when Dad launched his new beer. Mum laid on a publicity party, which was a success. Lots of people crowded the car park one afternoon as the barbecue got fired up. A photographer made me pose with Mum and Dad by the smoky charcoals. I tried hiding my face, but Mum pushed my chin up. In the end I could only stare back at the camera in misery. No chance to fetch Green, Dark & Shady. I shook nervously as the camera clicked.

The article about us appeared the next day, filling half a page and using a big photo. I looked very closely at the colour shot, like an animal seeing its reflection in a pool. My face was round and surly, my hair long and thick. But it was the red stripes of my childhood that gave me a shock. It was like someone had airbrushed them out. Sure, you could still see faint lines here and there, but nothing like the great scars I'd always imagined.

For years no one had been allowed to take my picture, or even wanted to. I went and had a look in the bathroom mirror, seeing myself anew. I took some more Samson photos with Dad's mobile, and put them on the computer, where I stared at them long and hard. But from every angle I was more human than I'd thought possible. I was finally seeing myself as real people would – not the slummers from school – and while I wasn't perfect, I wasn't so bad. Maybe even peachy, like Angel once said. So my heart began to heal.

Mum decided to let off steam one evening. We had just finished the dinner service, and the place had been full of boozers who'd read about us in the press.

Once again it was a bunch of brats who got Mum going as they ran around our play area. After a day of bright sunshine, I stood in the kitchen doorway watching my mother have fun. But she was too intense in her play, too eager to join in. She chased after the children on those elephant legs, shrieking with laughter. It frightened the smaller kids and they wouldn't let her get near. Some even ran away to the shelter of our fruit trees. It was sad, it was scary.

'I can see you,' she cried out to the hiding ones. And she was off into the orchard with all the grace of a rhino. She charged about as one nipper gave a nervous scream. I was about to give up on the scene in disgust when Mum came stumbling out under apple branches.

She stopped and swayed like a drunk, then fell forward into the sandpit. She sank to her knees and crashed onto one side. Even then I thought she was mucking about to amuse the kids, until she held her chest as if hit by bullets. And I raced across the car park towards her.

FORTY

'Lie still,' I said, kneeling beside her. 'Don't move.'

She was on her back now, her head cushioned by the sand. I tore off her third least favourite of my shirts and put it under her neck. The children all went howling to their parents, one of whom got busy on a mobile. Tipsy Sid came reeling across the yard, still holding a pint glass.

'Where's my dad?' I shouted.

'He's taken his new beer to Coniston,' said Sid. His voice was slurred. It sounded like he'd been running our bar for fun.

'Ring his mobile,' I said. 'Be quick.'

'Will do. There's an ambulance coming from Barrow.'

'It'll take ages. The roads are always packed.'

All the customers stood around in silence. Mum took a painful breath and I grabbed her hand, which was hot and still had scraps of bread dough on it. Her skin looked waxy and yellow-blue. The blood wasn't moving inside her like it should, and I knew we couldn't wait. Tearing away upstairs, I got a file that contained Standish's business card, which had survived the fire and my flight. I phoned one of his mobile numbers. He answered after two rings.

'Standish,' I said. 'I'm ready to deal, but I want something now. My mum's had a heart attack. Fly her to Barrow, and you get your stuff.' I already had a full folder tucked under my arm.

In the background a fax machine was beeping. Standish kept me waiting before he answered. 'Bring her here. We'll be ready.' He rang off as I sprinted back outside.

'Take her down to Harker!' I shouted at the throng. 'Who can do it?'

A guy with a beard and overalls grabbed me. 'My truck's got a tailgate,' he said, fumbling for his keys. He got in and backed his vehicle up to the sandpit. He lowered the hinged flap on the back, and we eased my mother onto it. As it rose, a dozen people piled in along with me. They were all strangers but nobody wanted to miss out.

'Mum,' I said. 'Can you hear me?'

She nodded very slowly, eyes closed, and breathed loudly.

'I won't leave you,' I said. 'Hold on.'

I sat beside her as we drove down the lane, turned right, then right again when we reached Harker Hall's driveway. The truck bombed along the path as I gave directions for the heli-pad, through the archway and onto the back lawn. The helicopter was revved and waiting. A pilot sat up front, the blades clacking above. Two men with a canvas stretcher got out and loaded Mum onto it, then into the chopper. It was like Standish had a whole team of lackeys on hand.

As he stood by me, I handed him the folder. Standish flipped through to check it was all for real, but even then I knew he wouldn't return here. I still had my own copies.

All I remember next is being high above Wolf Hill, inside the whirlybird. Standish sat up front with the pilot; both were wearing headphones to talk through. My mother lay quite still, being looked after by a white-skirted lady who'd found her way on board and told me she'd trained as a nurse.

We flew south towards Barrow, and for the first time I saw the Irish Sea from the air. There was a whole world beyond Cumbria's south-west coast of mudflats and sandy bays. A dark blue ocean lay waiting for me, lit by a sinking fireball.

Right under us, the main road that linked Broughton with Ulverston and Barrow was jammed with slow traffic. Many cars were towing motor boats, coming from the lakes near Ambleside, Coniston and Windermere. Heading the other way were those who'd spent their day on the shores of Silecroft, or at Barrow's nature reserves. Even if they all pulled over to the hedges, no ambulance could fight through with much speed. But the Standish helicopter flew like a snooty eagle over the mobs below.

Standish never once looked round to check on Mum, but stared out at the maze of greenery and grey villages. And before I knew it we were landing on a sports field close to Barrow hospital. A team of medics waited to cart Mum off to A&E. I rushed after them, not stopping to thank anyone, and the helicopter took flight again as quickly as it had come.

Dad arrived in a terrible panic, pressing his face to the window of a small room where Mum lay. He tried waving to her, his tears making the glass moist. At last they let him in when Mum had been made more stable. He came out two minutes later. 'Samson,' he said. 'She's asking for you. You haven't much time.'

He squeezed my fingers. A nurse led me into a room lit by clinical machines and overhead lights. Mum lay in bed, with tubes and gizmos stuck on her arms. She slowly rolled her head, and weakly held out a hand.

I nudged up a chair and sat down.

'Samson?' Her voice was faint.

'I'm here, Mum.'

The lines around her mouth were floppy. Her lips hardly moved as she whispered. 'Samson . . . I'm so sorry.'

'Don't be sorry, just get better.'

I leaned forward to hear my mother as trolleys clattered outside.

She whispered again. 'It nearly killed me!'

'Mum? What's that?'

'When you were born. It nearly ... killed me ... getting you ... out.'

'What? Oh, God!'

'Yes.' A smile crossed her face as she fought for breath. 'That's why ... I couldn't have any more ... I wanted ... so many ... Sorry I ... took it out on you.'

'It's OK. Honest.'

'No.' Mum's face twitched as she spoke through gasps. 'That's why ... I called you ... Samson ... I wanted you ... so strong ... for the kids I wouldn't have ... To bottle up some ... magic ... in a name.'

Now I smiled, and my eyes were wet. 'Maybe you did.'

She gripped my thumb like a child. 'You've got to be strong ... to help your dad. Even if I survive ... I can't go on ... Not like before ...'

'You'll survive. You will!'

'It's a risk ... Your dad needs you ... It's not what you wanted ... I know that ...'

'Whatever it takes,' I said.

Mum nodded, and brimmed over. 'Thank you,' she said. 'And I'm ... so sorry.'

'We're all equal now,' I said. 'There's nothing to be sorry for.'

Then a nurse and a young doctor bustled in. 'Time to leave,' said the nurse. 'Your mother's in good hands.'

I kissed Mum's flat hair and her wet hamster cheek,

then got shooed out. As my eyes filled up I tried to barge back in. 'Leave her be,' said Dad, holding my arm. 'She knows.'

FORTY-ONE

The operation went well, though I didn't ask for grisly details. They told us that if Mum had been left waiting at The Forge, her condition would've been far more risky.

I just kept our pub going, with help from Tipsy, as Dad spent his days and nights on hospital chairs. When he felt confident enough to come home, the first thing he did was send me down to Harker Hall with a free dinner invitation for the Standishes. He wanted to thank Standish, but I knew full well he'd refuse or find an excuse. There'd been nothing heroic in his rescue act.

But one shiny morning I trogged downhill with a note ready to shove in his letter box, and maybe catch a last glimpse of Angel.

As I took the right turning to go along the lane, a few vehicles came cruising towards me. They revved out of Harker Hall's driveway further down, and looked like removal or storage vans. I hid in the shade of that ivy cottage on the corner.

The first dusty truck went slowly by, and headed left up the narrow road past The Forge. Two others of a similar size drove through, then came a slight pause before the final motor. It was a white Mercedes, with Standish at the wheel. He wore his snazzy sun specs and was yakking away into a speaker phone. Lady Standish sat beside him, her face shaded by a wide pink hat.

I pressed myself against the cottage wall as the car crawled by. And there in the back was Angel, on the side nearest to me. She looked washed out, like all hope had long gone. She sat with hands in her lap, those hard blue eyes almost frozen. Her long hair was pure white as the sun blazed through it. Beside her, strapped in tightly, were the twins, playing some loud game with clapping hands.

'Angel,' I whispered. I took a few steps out of the ivy as Standish sped away uphill. When the car reached the first road bump I started walking after it, then jogged slowly. The white motor filled the whole lane, getting whipped by wild hedgerows. Even when it slowed up I could never reach it, although the twins caught sight of me and started shouting and pointing. But nobody else looked back. Angel's head never moved an inch.

The weather cooled down a bit as the summer wore on. Mum finally came home and sat outside in a comfy chair, close to the kitchen. She was able to call out orders and ideas to me as I worked away indoors.

'Samson, I've got a new recipe for an ice-cream pudding.'

'Oh, yeah?' I shouted. 'What's it like?'

'Well, it's quite an aphrodisiac. Plenty of cream and brandy in there. I've even got a name for it.'

'What's that then?'

'How about, Knicker Dropper Glory?'

'Outrageous!' I said.

But then she would spoil those peaceful moments by nagging. 'Samson! Why does this salad dressing taste like cyanide?'

'Uh, well I've been using hemp oil. It's all the rage.'

'It's vile. Go back to olive oil, and don't meddle.'

I thought the hemp taste was organic and funky, but I was learning to bite my tongue.

'And get that hair tied back in a ponytail. If you won't have it cut, at least keep it off your face.'

Which was a fair bargain of sorts.

At last I got that letter from the heritage fund, who seemed to like the idea of my charcoal project. They said it fitted in with their conservation ethics, so clearly no one there was taking money to trample on our traditions. Even when I rang and said the woodland needed some repairs after the fire, they were happy to carry on. There'd be funding on offer, depending on the scale of my business.

So I laid the Cumbrian Phoenix to rest, and he

remained a secret shared by just me and Angel, and maybe DJ Conscious Pilot. The police never hunted him again, as long as he didn't bother them. No one seemed to miss him too much.

I spent my days in the pub kitchen, learning just how hard Mum had worked over the years. We did well enough to employ extra help until the summer ended. Early one morning I was called outside by Dad, who said I had a visitor. And there stood Asha, the girl from the Coniston rave, with her brown skin and eastern eyes. The mole above her lip was still hairy. Her voice was all dreamy, making her sound a bit stoned.

'Hi,' she said. 'Remember me?'

'Uh, sure. Asha, right?'

'Yeah. So, is that protest camp still going on here?'

'Ah. No, not really. I kinda fought off the destroyers.'

'You did?' She toyed with the coloured threads in her hair. 'Cool. I'm just, like, travelling around right now. Is there anywhere I can crash, maybe somewhere outdoors? I've got a tent.'

'Sure,' I said. 'There's the pick of my woodland, and even a tree house. You wanna see?'

Asha took up her rucksack and followed me. On the way I told her about my news from the heritage funders. I took her to the pitstead and showed her Cherry's old hut, talking away about charcoal burns. Asha looked at me like I was some kind of eco superhero, which I didn't mind at all.

'There's a lot to do,' I said. 'We've got our work cut out, if you're staying.'

'Where's that Angel? I thought you were together.'

'Gone. Long gone.' And I told her about the real Victoria Standish, and the recent fire. 'In a way she did me a favour,' I said. 'That blaze cut away some of the underbrush, which feeds a wildfire if another one starts. It cleared some of the litter off the forest floor – grasses, needles, small shrubs. And it might have burned out a few bad insects and diseases.'

My memory of Angel faded as Asha walked around, her long skirt whirling with rainbow colours. She took off her trainers and walked barefoot through Appletree to the giant redwood, through the surviving flowers.

We climbed up onto the cosy ledge I'd helped Angel build. 'It's neat here,' said Asha. 'Well neat.'

'Yeah, and listen, you can come to The Forge for the bathroom and stuff.'

Asha lay back like a hippy princess, her long brown legs the colour of hazel branches. 'Cool,' she said. 'Well cool.'

And so it was.

I left her to settle in and walked back into blackened woodland. Someone from the Forestry Commission was coming to fell the charred trees and help me plant new ones. As I reached the hut, I saw something else that had survived the fire. My charcoal angel, still in two halves on the ground. I threw them onto the pitstead, and was walking home when a sudden voice seemed to call me back.

Not so fast, lad.

I slowed up with a smile. 'Cherry Ashburner. Not heard from you awhile.'

Aye, you've been fair busy. What about those hazel trees your mad girlfriend put a match to?

'They'll survive. I've been reading up on how to save the old growths. Anyhow, I can always use beech or oak for now.'

Black trunks rose skyward all about me, including pines and alders, some of which had been nursed by Cherry himself.

Hmm. Best keep an eye on this new bird that's flown into your nest.

'Asha? Nah, she's here to help.'

Oh, aye? Got a nice moley lump over her gob. You'll have fun chewing on that.

A pack of rats poked their noses out of a burned shrub. Most of the wildlife would have fled the fire, though some must have perished.

'We're none of us perfect, Cherry. Me above all. See you, then.'

Right enough. I'll be here if you need me.

FORTY-TWO

A few evenings later, I met an old fellow looking over towards Appletree Wood. His eyes were dewy with age, and he leaned on a stick by the drystone wall. Behind us stood a deserted Harker Hall, its windows dark and closed.

The man coughed, and wiped his runny nose. 'It's a grand view,' he said. We looked beyond the barley field, where the edge of my charred wood lay dark green in the distance. A swirl of rooks flew from the gap above the pitstead, like nursery rhyme blackbirds escaping from a pie.

'Yeah,' I said. 'It's grand.'

A blue sports car pulled up behind us, heading into Harker Hall. I had nailed a copy of Cherry's old document to the steel farm gate there. A guy in his twenties got out to open the gate, a white cricket sweater around his neck. He had thick dark hair swept back down to his shoulders, and smart jeans. He tore my title deed off the nail, and read it.

'OK there, mate?' I called over.

'Hi,' he said. 'The name's Harker. Nigel Harker.' By now the old man had wandered off along the lane and was turning uphill in The Forge's direction.

I took a few steps across. 'Samson Ashburner. The owner of that document.'

Nigel Harker read the page through again, then folded it. 'We've just bought the hall back off Lord Standish,' he said. 'I didn't want to see it leave the family in the first place. My elder brother screwed up there. So when it came on the market I was keen to get it back.'

He seemed a decent enough guy. 'Nice car,' I said, though I hated them.

'Thanks. But look here at the wording of this document. I'm afraid you've misread it. Listen. It says that after Cherry's death, the woodland will be handed down to the youngest child of *the family*.'

'So?'

'So, it doesn't say whose family that means,' said Nigel. 'Harker or Ashburner. I'm the youngest in my family. That could make the woodland mine. Looks like those old guys were sozzled when they wrote this.'

Nigel cast a mischievous look over the fields towards Appletree. 'Make a cracking site for an off-roading park up there,' he said. 'Clear those trees first. Plenty of rough ground for big motors to go wild on. I bet the earth gets good and muddy. Maybe it could double as a car rally course.'

He snapped off a thin branch, then drew a large oval shape in the gravel. He traced his twig through the dirt, making loud engine noises. 'Yeah! And I could put a café in the top corner. Right up by that old bridleway. Maybe get a McDonald's in.'

I felt a familiar surge of fury. 'I'll fight you for it,' I warned, my voice trembling. 'Tooth and nail.'

Nigel smiled and slapped my shoulder. 'I'm only kidding. What are your plans for it, anyway?'

I blew out my cheeks with relief and told him about the heritage grant. 'Sounds great,' said Nigel, sitting against his bonnet. He spread his hands like a business-man selling himself to the world. 'Organic charcoal from the Harker Estate!'

I turned the idea over. 'Yeah. I might call it that.'

Nigel bounced off his car, and opened the driver's door. 'I could handle the business side, if you knock the stuff out.'

'Deal,' I said. I even opened the gate so my new partner's car could purr along the driveway. I walked after him, and helped him unpack a few bags, including a swanky golfing set. He talked on as we went around the back, near the great lawn, which was filled with roses. The helicopter landing pad was a rough circle of clay. Nigel stopped and looked at the outbuildings, dotted around like small cottages.

'Lord Harker, who wrote this paper, was my great-grandpa. That means our great-grandpas were partners too.'

It was a weird feeling. Three generations of our families had lived and died to bring me and Nigel full circle. We were the modern Cherry and Henry, now ready to make new history within Appletree.

Nigel took the copied document off me. He said, 'We never thought that Appletree went with Harker Hall anyway. But when Standish saw the architect's plans, drawn up when the woodland was Henry Harker's, he assumed that it did. Or maybe he just realized the potential and took a gamble. What the old plans wouldn't mention was this deed made by our ancestors. It looks legal and binding enough to me.'

I gazed at the grey bricks of Harker Hall, and the outbuildings that once housed Lord Henry's workforce. I wondered which room Angel had slept in during her stay.

'Anyway, don't worry,' said Nigel. 'It's old families like mine that are keeping these landscapes safe. Not your new guns like Standish. I say, you fancy a beer?'

I turned to him with a smile. 'Sure. Come to our pub.'

'What? It's your family who owns that place?' Nigel struck his head. 'Of course, the Ashburners, like Ashburner's Wood. Is the beer as good as ever?'

'Yeah, and Dad's made one of his own now. A light summer bitter.'

'Sounds good. What's it called?'

'It's called Ashburner's Phoenix,' I said. 'Appropriate.'

We strolled up the lane to The Forge, my hooded top around my waist. Green & Shady were tucked away in

Dark's pockets now. As we came in sight of the pub and its thick orchard, Nigel stopped.

'So, partner,' he said. 'If we're gonna honour that deed in good faith, where's my cherry brandy? It says in the document that you'll always keep our family supplied. You've gotta fulfil your part of the bargain.'

We took a stroll through the fruity grove, among apples and damsons, to the wild cherry trees near the back. Their flowers were white, the red fruit ripening among the branches. I plucked a few and they were sweet on the tongue. There would be enough each summer to make several bottles of liqueur. And given my dad's troubled history of brewing, this could be a nice quiet job for my mother. Wolf Hill Cherry Brandy, made on the premises, from the harvest of our very own orchard.

I couldn't wait to tell Mum about this. It was time she taught everyone how to 'Drink the View'.